The somewhat pink face was earnest and tense. Morton had the uneasy feeling that Marriott believed what he was saying. He said, "Look, captain, if you're trying for peace here, I'm on your side. I want negotiations to resume—and if you've made headway where we haven't, hell, man, I'll get behind you and push. For God's sake, don't be secretive. Tell me what's wrong and I'll cooperate to solve the wrongness."

Abruptly the face on the ViewComm was sarcastic. "What's happened here," said Marriott, "stirs men to other darker emotions than cooperation. What happened is that as a result of an identity confusion you have replaced me as head of the Irsk government. Of the darkness, in short. What do you think of *that?*"

No ordeal changes the nature of man and no crisis changes the nature of states.

Charles de Gaulle

THE
DARKNESS
ON
DIAMONDIA

A. E. van Vogt

DAW BOOKS, INC.

DONALD A. WOLLHEIM, PUBLISHER
1633 Broadway, New York NY 10019

Cover art by Wayne D. Barlowe

DEDICATION

To Fred Pohl who for better or worse in 1964, when he was editor of *Galaxy*, *Worlds of If*, and *Worlds of Tomorrow*, persuaded me to write science fiction again.

FIRST DAW PRINTING, APRIL 1982

1 2 3 4 5 6 7 8 9

DAW TRADEMARK REGISTERED
U.S. PAT. OFF. MARCA
REGISTRADA. HECHO EN U.S.A.

PRINTED IN U.S.A.

One

"GRAY THOUGHTS," Morton read, "under a gray sky . . .
Across the darkening roofs of New Naples, Christomene
watched from her window Vesuvius II sputtering and smoking with a tireless endurance. She let her thoughts take form
in the distance, in the uneven flow of smoke, like a person
looking for pictures in a dancing log fire."

At that point he paused in his reading, because the car hit
a bomb-filled hole; and, besides, that was about the limit of
his attention span on anything since his arrival on Diamondia
VI.

Morton closed his eyes momentarily, and surreptitiously
(he hoped) squeezed them hard several times, striving once
more to force the hovering darkness out of his brain. The
brief effort, to be repeated hundreds of times in the course of
the day, brought relief for the ten thousandth time since he
had landed with the Negotiating Committee.

Suddenly, as if a weight had lifted, the darkness drew
back. Instantly, he felt brighter inside; normal again. He
glanced over at Lieutenant Bray, who was driving. He had
heard in a vague fashion that the dynamic Intelligence officer,
now attached to the New Naples command, did fiction writing. But this was the first time he had seen a sample.

"Does this kind of involved imagery really sell?" Morton
asked, picking up again the thread of what he had been doing
before the darkness descended on him.

Bray's thin, intense face assumed a cautious expression. "I
never know," he confessed. "I've sold about thirty exactly like
that. But then about thirty others, also exactly like that, have
come back.

"My own idea," he went on, "is that it all depends on how
much the editor on Earth is bowled over by receiving the
yarn direct from the, uh, exotic city in which it is laid. This
one will be posted New Naples, Diamondia."

Morton nodded and realized that he was smiling for the
first time in many a long day. "What's the plot?" he asked.

5

"A Diamondian heiress," said the lieutenant, "caught in the turmoil of war falls for an Earth soldier—of course, he's really a millionaire who came over as a private because he's that kind of a guy; and she never did approve of the war."

Morton tried to picture that and couldn't. Then he tried to picture the steel-brained Lieutenant Bray grinding out the necessary words. That drew an even bigger blank. He leaned back in the seat. "Why don't you write about the work we're doing here?" he said.

Lieutenant Bray sighed. "People always ask me that. But truth is, it lacks glamour. What you and I are here for—to get Earth federation armies out of this war—is too ugly. We know perfectly well the Irsk will murder all the human beings on Diamondia when we're gone. So I'm hoping to get this story sold before that happens."

Morton said quickly but halfheartedly, "There's no proof that the Irsk will massacre anybody."

That was the official line; and he had to say it as a matter of mechanically doing his duty. Which was about what one man could do. Even someone who was on the Negotiating Committee staff, as he was.

Bray was speaking again. "Take this girl, Isolina Ferraris, whom you're going to visit. She's pretty enough, I suppose, if you like that kind of thing. And I understand she had an Italian mother from Earth, who died shortly after giving birth to Isolina. Theoretically, that should make her a perfect heroine. But what is the truth? She's a Diamondian nationalist. She uses her body as a weapon. Everybody is so desperate and afraid that things we like to think of as being true about human beings have gone out of the window. But her father is a contact in this area with the underground group. So we have to deal with a mad young woman."

He shrugged; then: "An added point is that the whole terrified outfit is assassinating dissenters right and left, and they don't trust us. Back home, folks like to believe that the mass of the Diamondians are sensible people, who will peacefully give up their lives so backhomers can stop paying such high taxes."

"And so they are, generally, sensible," said Morton. To himself he added, "We keep trusting."

"Not this bunch, colonel," the lieutenant said. "Imagine a plot with a hundred low characters in it, all egotistical, all scoundrels, thinking only of themselves and not of the poor, overburdened taxpayers of the federation. And not one of

6

'em capable of making the noble sacrifice that the heiress in my story—"

Bray stopped in midsentence, made a dangerous swerve in that heavy traffic but managed to pull over to a parking position beside a red curb. He did not even glance at Morton. Sitting there, his body rigid, he sat and squeezed his eyes several times.

Morton watched him in stunned silence, thinking, just like I've been doing.

Bray seemed to be recovering, and, belatedly, Morton realized that he would have to show awareness of the astonishing thing the other man had done.

"What's the matter?" he asked.

The younger man seemed to shrink down into the seat. Yet he said in that familiar, firm voice of his, "I intended to talk to you about this today, sir. Was glad, in fact, that we were going out together so I could have the opportunity. Since my condition varies in intensity, I waited for a severe recurrence. And you just saw it."

"Condition?" echoed Morton in a neutral tone.

A long pause. Then:

"Something periodically moves in on me," said Bray.

"What exactly happens?" asked Morton. Involuntarily he held his breath, waited for an answer, tense, intent, unwary.

"Well—" Bray seemed uncertain.

"Is it—is it like a . . . darkness?" asked Morton.

"That's it!" Bray verbally pounced on the description. "It's as if something, another entity, is reaching in . . ." He paused, uncertain again.

Morton's thoughts flashed to his own darkness. And he considered its nature in the light of the word Bray had used. *Entity*. He thought: Good God, can it be?

It was a moment of disaster and abrupt fear. To save himself, he did his old thing: looked around, oriented himself.

Surprisingly hard to do. Because this time the effort was almost as automatic as the inner disturbance which made it necessary. Yet he was aware that they were still on the Via Roma. All around were the madly charging vehicles driven by people with bright, cheerful eyes and vaguely smiling faces.

Watching the traffic through his own glazed eyes, Morton began to feel better. His pounding heart slowed. The fear dimmed. He realized that he was examining the *entity* not as a new calamity but as an old problem about which he had been offered some additional insights.

7

. . . He grew aware that Lieutenant Bray was speaking again and that in that normally determined voice there was the barest touch of grief.

"I keep intending," said the young man, "to report in for psychiatric examination. But then I think, how the hell will that look on my record? And I can't bring myself to do it."

Morton, who had had a few fleeting impulses himself in the direction of medical aid, nodded his acceptance of the reason. Actually, the situation was worse than Bray feared. Such matters, he knew from his higher echelon position, were handled by a grim routine. Psychiatrists on remote planets were usually young people; and they had been taught not to try to cure anybody and risk their reputations. So off to some base hospital on another world went the unsuspecting—until that too late moment—victim. What happened to him and his career after that was cringe-level data for anyone who learned of it afterward.

He was inclined to believe that Bray—and perhaps even he himself—were not high enough echelon to evade such a fate.

Thinking about such factual matters was sobering. Suddenly he was aware not only of the traffic but of their location. "There's the museum just ahead," Morton said. "Pull up in front of it and let me off. I'll walk the rest of the way."

As Bray started the car again and gingerly edged forward, Morton said to him, "And don't mention your condition to anyone until you have talked to me about it further. Don't go near a psychiatrist."

Bray nodded mutely, his eyes alertly watching the traffic. But a minute or so later when he had pulled up as instructed, he said in a troubled voice, "Colonel, are you sure you should visit this girl by yourself? These Diamondians are the damnedest bunch of assassins you ever heard of."

"We're their only hope," Morton answered. "Persuading us to stay is all they've got. Everybody knows you can't ship lift half a billion people off a planet. So they'd better not make us mad."

Bray continued to scowl unhappily. "May I ask, sir, what is our purpose in dealing at all with this General Ferraris gang?"

"Well," Morton began.

And then he stopped, momentarily blank.

What bothered him was the recollection that he actually had no clear-cut instructions from Paul Laurent, who headed the Negotiating Committee. Laurent had simply said to him, "Basically, Charles, there's nothing for us to do. Our commit-

8

tee title is a misnomer. The word 'Negotiating' is not relevant, because we're here to get the Earth federation forces off this planet, and we're going to do that whether or not anyone negotiates with us. But nonetheless, act *as if* negotiation is our purpose. That way we may actually get something settled here."

He'd become vague about those words. Somehow, Morton thought, as he sat there beside Bray, I'm already more involved than those instructions permit. He wanted, he realized, negotiations to solve the deadly problem on Diamondia.

Aloud slowly, he said, "Don't be too cynical, lieutenant. And don't assume all of these groups are equally murderous. General Ferraris and his daughter, according to my report— and that is why I'm here—have contacted a large, representative Irsk group, and have dispatched a sizable peace delegation. I'd like us to discover the details of that transaction, and it occurred to me, why don't I just go over and ask?"

Bray said, "Oh!"

Morton changed the subject, saying matter-of-factly, "You turn off here." He pointed. "La Strada dell'Arenaccio is just beyond the botanical gardens. Drive along it until you come to Capodochino Corapo, I can't remember how many miles—eight, maybe. I'll join you there later tonight for the visit to the Ferraris farm. Starting noon tomorrow we watch the junction at Corapo and in the afternoon stop certain cars. According to our information, the people in them will be the returning peace delegation."

He almost added, "I hope," but restrained himself. Instead he said, "And don't forget our purpose is not to screw up peace negotiations but to find out their nature. If we use our enforcement technology correctly, we can count on the members of the peace delegation not revealing that we stopped them . . . Their self-esteem." He broke off. "My guess is that a solution on Diamondia will have a very high finite logic number. Meaning reason will not be involved. As for Captain Marriott, he's in charge at Corapo. Whose side is he on? We need to know."

Bray said he would do his best to find out. But his voice as he said it was not very interested. And in his face was a new thought. He looked baffled. "Sir," he said abruptly, "it is now nearly two thousand years since technology and science began in earnest. Yet here in 3819 A.D., Man is still obstreperous and unthinking. By this time why isn't there a pill that we can give all these mad Diamondians and civilize them?"

Morton had to smile though the question wrenched him from his previous thoughts. "I have an answer," he said. "I don't know if it's *the* answer."

"What is it?"

"Man thinks with what used to be called modern logic. But his basic nature, like the universe, operates on finite logic."

"Well—" shrugged Bray, "I suppose you're right."

But his youthful face showed continuing dissatisfaction, and he moved his body in a way that anticipated that Morton would now leave the car.

Morton didn't move. He was astonished to realize that there was actually an opposite purpose in him.

My discovery that Bray also has a darkness in his mind is an Intelligence event of preemptive importance. Could it be that somebody had a machine focused on Bray and himself?

So far it didn't seem dangerous. But the fact that two people in Intelligence were affected had to be significant.

Can the darkness wait on other events? It cannot! The Diamondian nationalists had to come second to the thing in Bray's head and his. For example, he must find out at once if other people were having a similar experience.

. . . Bray's voice came in on his thoughts, sounding slightly remote, "What's the matter, sir?"

Morton was instantly warned by that sudden sense of farawayness. Another of his numerous battles with the entity was about to transpire.

He spoke hurriedly, "Cancel the orders I just gave you, lieutenant. The girl can wait. What you've just told me about that thing in your head interests me. Drive me back to headquarters."

As he spoke the words, he realized that the mass of blackness moving in was extra large, as occasionally happened. He braced himself.

And that was the last thing he later remembered doing.

Two

FOR LIEUTENANT BRAY, the visible event, then, was: the man in the seat beside him suddenly went limp. As Bray gazed, wide-eyed, Morton's body slowly slid down under the dashboard. The head ended up leaning, mouth open, with the

10

neck against the seat itself. There, all hunched up, with no further room to move, it remained jammed in.

At that point, and not an instant earlier—

My God, Bray thought, *he's been assassinated.*

Horrified, he ducked down beside the still body of his superior. He crouched there, permitting himself no further reaction. Simply, he recorded through his senses.

The warm, warm wind, with the name Bray could never remember, was blowing across the car from the direction of the bay. It brought with it some of the perpetual heat from the continent a hundred miles away over the water and brought, too, something of the dampness of the water above which it had passed.

It occurred to the sweating Bray that if there had been an energy sound in connection with the killing, he would never have heard it. Even a pistol shot—which was more likely in old-fashioned New Naples—would have got swallowed up in the hum and the throb and the roar of the passing cars.

He deduced then that no one else had even noticed the disaster. Crouching there, he realized: It's up to me.

With that awareness, his finger sought the catch on the little hook under the dashboard. Pulled it like a trigger. As might a sliding door, the flexible graphite-fiber top came gliding up from its bed and clicked into place.

Instantly he was safe from all except overwhelm impacts. And so for the first time he examined the body, looking for a wound.

Found nothing.

But he realized that the older man was breathing.

He's alive.

Bray had already straightened up. Now he opened the door on his side of the machine, jumped out, ran around to the other side and jerked open that door. Moments later, he had dragged Morton out of the car and had him lying full length on the sidewalk.

He was now able to verify that the older man had suffered no wounds, and that his heart was beating normally and his breathing was regular.

But there was no sign of returning consciousness.

Nonetheless, the young officer began to feel up. To Bray the world was what it was, no more and no less, no better and no worse. Diamondia was no exception. He climbed to his feet, and he stood there beside the unconscious body; and he felt no sense of urgency or special concern now that he knew it was an alive body.

'Even in unconsciousness, Bray observed, Morton looked strong. His face muscles held their firm shape. Lying there, the older man was the epitome of a determined person struck down but waiting. His was a handsome face, and a lean (but not too lean) body. Bray himself an active product of a muscle buildup regimen, was both thinner and, of course, younger.

Yet in his association with Morton, he had occasionally accidentally bumped, jostled, or run into the older man . . . and each time had almost literally bounced. He surmised Morton to be in his late thirties and at an optimum balance of maturity and good health. Which made what had now happened just a little sad.

Thinking thus but not letting it dim him, Bray whistled softly and watched the people who went by on the sidewalk. At first they were all Diamondians. They had, if anything, a blond Scandinavian or even English cast of countenance. And they were not about to involve themselves in his problem.

Bray mentally conducted several silent conversations from the Diamondian point of view.

Look at that federation officer lying there.

I see him. He's a member of the Negotiating Committee. Notice that special shoulder insignia.

Then to hell with him, signor.

And again:

See that poor officer.

Don't get involved, my friend. Before you know it, you also will be on the non-negotiating Negotiating Committee, wasting your time as they are wasting theirs.

Finally:

Is he dead, I wonder.

Let us hope so. Maybe that will give these federation rascals the feel of what it's going to be like here on Diamondia after they're gone.

It seemed to Bray that something like that must be going through the minds of the Diamondians who hurried by in either direction. They merely glanced at Morton and himself and otherwise paid no attention.

The Diamondians, he knew from personal contact, were quite bitter about the Negotiating Committee. Often their bitterness took the form of cutting humor, occasionally instant rage and sometimes instant murder.

All this was apart from the assassins.

As Bray stood there, undecided as to what he should do, two Irsk came walking along. They wore the green-striped

12

shirts of Friends of the Diamondians over their heavy under-clothing, and they good-naturedly helped him lift Morton into the back seat of the car.

Thereupon, both volunteered to go along and assist him in taking Morton to the army hospital.

Bray shook his head. It was an automatic rejection based on his own evaluation of the Irsk-Diamondian situation. No doubt millions of Irsk on this portion of the biggest of the three Diamondian continents were exactly what they seemed to be: the easygoing, tentacled beings, who had been found here in vast numbers by the first colonists, living peacefully among the ruins of their ancient civilization.

From the beginning they showed good nature and good-will. Irsk were always volunteering to help a human being perform a task. And when Earth federation commissions later investigated the consequences, they found that the Diamondians had permitted Irsk helpers to take over first the task of assisting and then the whole job. The early investigators merely shook their heads in wondering concern as they departed. However, a later group salved everybody's conscience by ordering that equal wages be paid the Irsk.

The results of *that* were astonishing. At first the natives didn't know what to do with the money. Then they began to eat the Diamondian food. They had had no visible source of food previously. But suddenly they were eating pizza, hot dogs, cheese, macaroni and hamburgers. The restaurant business boomed. And as they munched, their peculiar (in the eyes of Diamondians) long faces remained wreathed in a perpetual grimace, which—it was decided—was their way of smiling.

The two Irsk, who had just helped Bray, had that smile. But all Irsk were no longer trustworthy; not even a percentage of those who wore the green-striped shirts. So—by Bray's reasoning—none were.

After all, he thought, the Irsk might be slyly happy to assist the Negotiating Committee . . . so long as no negotiations were going on.

Aloud, Bray said politely, "Thank you very much, but my friend and I will be all right, I'm sure."

The two Irsk made courteous sounds in their soft voices and walked on, looking back several times, smiling. Bray, his mind suddenly made up, got into the car.

He did not drive to the Federation hospital.

He was no fool. More than a week before, he had first noticed Morton surreptitiously squeeze his eyes. He observed

13

that his superior always tried to turn away at the moment of eye squeeze. It was a five minute pattern, Bray discovered. He practiced closing his own eyes at five minute intervals, first timing himself, then guessing.

Couldn't do it. He could never estimate five minutes exactly. Something extremely automatic was periodically closing Morton's eyes. For several days Bray considered what he could say that would detour the older man from being as smart as he usually was.

Now he was shocked. He had offered a wildly imaginative thought. Within minutes Morton had squeezed his eyes again and in the very act had become unconscious. The question was, under these varying circumstances what was best for Morton?

There was no best. There was simply the need to wait, at least for a while. How long? That was not clear.

Feeling philosophical, completely brave and hopeful that he might learn something more, Bray set the car in motion and was soon another insane driver in the mad traffic of New Naples.

Arrived in Corapo—as the Diamondians would say—safe by the miracle of God, Bray parked his car near but not exactly at the Earth federation military post. Whereupon he shadowed the transparent panels of the sides, front and rear. This effectively blocked any view from the outside of Morton's body. And, of course, the car itself, locked, was a relatively secure place for an unconscious human being. Also, it was gimmicked for extra safety.

The sun was already quite low in the western sky as Bray turned away from the car and started along the narrow sidewalk of the winding street. His destination was a building that he had, until now, merely glanced at in order to locate the sign that identified it as the Earth federation post.

Out of the car, away from his thoughts about Morton, no longer intent on mere location, Bray took a second look.

And stopped.

The post was a severe-looking, one-story structure, which did not fit in with the old-fashioned architecture of the rest of the town. Local culture buffs must have been outraged; so even if his memory wasn't already stirring, he would have deduced that there was a special reason why it had been constructed as it was. Bray wondered if Morton knew that such a building existed on Diamondia.

He himself had heard vaguely of such structures. That they were built of special materials, that they showed their unusual qualities by the way they reacted to threat, and that they were normally used only on planets where maximum security was a must. Diamondia VI had been put in such a category . . .

As he moved forward again, it occurred to Bray that it was odd that Marriott, a suspected man, was in charge of *this*.

At the door, uniformed guards saluted Bray lackadaisically. Which presumably meant that they were emotionally involved with the Diamondian dilemma. Such individuals, if reported, would be returned to civilian life when they left the planet. The armed forces couldn't use men who lost their *élan* for any reason.

True, he was emotionally concerned also. But tests had shown that he could mentally step back from his own feelings and actually seek a solution to a problem; and not himself become a part of the problem, which is what Morton believed Marriott had done.

After walking along a gleaming, brightly lighted corridor, Bray found Marriott in his private office at the rear of the building. The commanding officer of the Corapo unit was a tall, fairly good-looking man with dark hair, who greeting Bray curtly: "I thought I'd have dinner brought in here, lieutenant, where we can talk without fear of being overheard. And now, lieutenant, how about some good Diamondian wine."

The double naming of his rank in a single statement made Bray hopeful. It encouraged the belief that Morton had sized up Marriott correctly, and that it had been subtly wise to send *Lieutenant* Bray ahead to have dinner with *Captain* Marriott by the reasoning that the latter would be disarmed by the fact of his superior status.

They drank wine. They had dinner. They drank more wine. That was the early evening.

Bray, who had a stomach akin to metallic crystal, nevertheless progressively pretended to be intoxicated.

Bray was—he had to admit it—puzzled by the older man. Marriott had a long back history on Diamondia, for a non-Diamondian. Intelligence records said he had first arrived on the planet at age twenty-six. He was apparently content at that time to teach in one or another Diamondian university.

The Irsk rebellion began four years after his arrival and had now been at its present violent level for ten years.

Which made James Marriott forty years old.

He looked his age. Little red lines of dissipation showed in his face. He had been a woman chaser from the first day of his arrival. It was on his record that he had once jocularly remarked that "Diamondian women are too desperate to be married. You've got to be a tough, bachelor type to stand the strain."

Subsequent account showed him to have switched to prostitutes as soon as they began to turn up on the streets in large numbers after the civil war began.

Surprisingly, he volunteered his services to the Earth federation forces. It was surprising in view of his hedonistic history. Top command was delighted to have a highly trained individual, who also knew Diamondia. Corapo seemed the wrong place for such a person to have dead ended. Equally wrong was the earnestness with which he now plied Lieutenant Lester Bray with an excess of liquid refreshment.

What was he up to? The question, it seemed to Bray, needed to be asked. Silently, he asked it. There was no answer.

It was quite dark when Marriott said, "I don't think we should wait any longer. They're expecting us, and Diamondians place a high evaluation on courtesy."

Bray surged to his feet. Next, he staggered across the room. From the corner of his eye, he saw that Marriott was watching him with unconcealed contempt. Deliberately, Bray almost fell; but when Marriott caught him and helped him through the door, he shoved the aiding hand aside, protesting with a drunken confidence, "I'll be all right."

The two men emerged into the open from the rear of the post. Bray, though he pretended to be unaware, saw that they were inside a wire fence enclosure, which contained a number of small armored cars, guarded by a single sentinel. After Marriott and the soldier had assisted Bray into one of the vehicles, the captain leaned in and said, "I have to go back for something. Make yourself comfortable. Should only take a minute." Having spoken, he closed the door.

He was absent at least ten minutes. During that time Bray made enough tests, while maintaining his drunken appearance for the benefit of the guard, to establish that all the steel hard doors of the sturdy machine were locked. For a few minutes that bothered him. He wondered if he could (if necessary) shoot his way out with his pistol.

The return of Marriott ended those speculations. The tall, dark-haired man climbed in beside him and started the motor. He made no apology for his long absence.

On the way to the Ferraris farm Bray sang a little and muttered certain philosophical remarks about the fact that

16

there were probably no really important events in any one area of the universe.

"It's just energy," he murmured. "A human being is just a closed circuit energy unit."

And in less than a hundred years every such unit now living—"manifesting" was the word used by Bray—would have drained off into the surrounding space-time continuum.

Bray pointed out owlishly that the history of such energy interactions were usually written down by the individual closed circuits. These also tended to fade or become confused with the passage of time.

"So," said Bray airily—he sang it in a stuttering voice—"it really doesn't matter if the Irsk presently scatter into cosmic dust the result of every act of lust on Dia-mo-nd-i-a."

By the time he was singing this song, he was sprawled on a couch in a large room in the Ferraris farmhouse, vaguely aware that around him were at least a dozen people, mostly men. The vagueness derived from his eyes being closed most of the time, as if he were having a hard time staying awake. But he was also puzzled. He could understand why he was here. Morton was extremely anxious to discover the truth about Marriott. But it was not easy to decide why the Diamondians had been willing to give a whole evening to a visitor who by now they must consider the most obnoxious drunkard they had ever seen.

Would these hot-blooded Diamondians react violently? Bray visualized his body collapsed in a posture that looked just about as revoltingly relaxed as he could manage; and it seemed to him that some penalty would be invoked presently.

Near him, as he thought that, there was movement. Then . . .

Bray was aware of a silence. Finally someone bent over him.

It was the moment he had been waiting for. He bit into the hard seed he had held in his mouth for just this purpose. It broke onto his tongue with a faint sound. The drop of liquid that was there almost at once dissolved into the most foul-smelling gas. Though Bray had practiced many times the act of spitting it out, he still gagged as he belched it forth.

As usual, he felt sorry for the person into whose face the gas discharged. Above him, there was a hoarse masculine noise of distress. Somebody staggered and almost fell. Then, a man—it seemed like the same distressed person—cursed vigorously.

A woman's loud whisper admonished him. But obviously

17

the man had been convinced by the stench that Bray's mouth had emitted. He said loudly, "Don't worry about him."

Bray snored.

Another man said, "So that's what we're depending on to help save us."

A woman's footsteps came near Bray—Isolina, Bray guessed—and she said in a rather youthful voice: "He seems scarcely out of his teens to be such a drunken bumb."

A man said, "The Negotiating Committee had to select the scum of the service in order to get anyone who would be willing to stand by while five hundred million people were exterminated."

It was the voice of Jimmy Marriott.

And so, thought Bray, *I've just heard the ideal that made him a collaborator.*

Having heard the damning words, knowing that Captain James Marriott was in fact what had been suspected, he had accomplished his own purpose. There remained the task of getting out of here with a whole skin.

"Where's the other one?" said the young woman's voice. "He was supposed to come and see me this afternoon—"

So it was Isolina.

"—But," the girl continued, "those who were watching for him reported that he became unconscious and was lying on the sidewalk a hundred yards from the house. No one knows what happened to him after he was put back in the car—"

"Don't worry about Morton." It was Marriott, casually. "He was in this bum's car, and I've had him taken to a hospital. If I can work it, I'll have this one carted over there, also."

"You mean—"

Marriott laughed. "Yes. With instructions to our people there to ship them to some base hospital far away."

A man sighed. "That is the easiest method. I had an awful feeling Morton was getting close, and that we'd have to do something."

A rough hand grabbed Bray's leg. "Help me with this creature," said Jim Marriott's voice.

It was a sudden action, a sudden nearness—and Bray almost jumped. He actually felt a reflex, and managed to convert it into a hostile foot gesture and a muttering about human beings having been on Diamondia only three hundred years pretending during all that time to be Earthmen.

But in this year of our lord 3819 A.D., it was long established that it was hard to find a true Earthman even on

18

Earth. Diamondians had undoubtedly eaten enough hamburgers, and they were to be commended for trying to re-create the ancient Earth culture, but alas the real, gay, delightful Earth of old had been lost somewhere in a millennia of racial mixing.

Still, it was better to have Diamondians pretending to be Earthmen than to have no men following the old Earth tradition.

So sang Bray.

His singing and his muttering seemed to be considered normal for a drunk. He was lifted and carried out and put in Marriott's vehicle. And so he had time to realize with a lot of dismay what he had heard said about Morton. It was astonishing to realize that watchers had been fanned out from the Ferraris town house as far away as the Via Roma and the museum.

He had another, more pensive thought. Was it possible that Marriott had himself taken Morton out of Bray's car? Maybe—Bray was suddenly hopeful—that was where the physicist had gone during his ten minute disappearance.

If Marriott had done the deed himself, then it was one of those marvelous coincidences, or rather fortuitous acts that Intelligence officers dreamed of in visualizing perfect solutions to their problems. Like all officer level cars of the Intelligence service, Bray's was gimmicked. Among other protective things, it was set to put forth a hypnotizing frequency, which had on it a single confusing command for the person who actually bent close to the lock at the moment of forced entry.

Undoubtedly, if Marriott had been that person, there must have been helpers to do the work of lifting Morton's body. Tests had long ago established that the hypnotized person could not during his period of temporary confusion do the job himself.

Did he remember the experience? There was no sign of it.

But it might provide a future hold on the captain.

Bray's thought ended because the people were gathering around the car.

"I don't understand." It was the voice of Isolina Ferraris. "What is the point of shipping these two off the planet?"

A man chuckled. "It's just a game, dear. We don't really care what happens to these two pawns. They're nothing."

"We'll be nothing, too, before very long," said Isolina. "So what's the point? Two nothings striking each other with

19

shadow swords. If this is your idea of a joke—" Her voice went up. "Release these men!"

"Oh, for the sake of God, Isolina."

"You know my policy," the girl said in that youthful voice. "Do absolutely nothing irrational any more. No more unnecessary battles out of rage. You people told me this was an important matter, that very likely the Intelligence department of the Negotiating Committee had become aware of the departure of our peace delegation to meet with those friendly Irsk and was trying to find out its bearing on their mission. Now you tell me I've wasted an evening on two nothings."

"Well, it's not really that—" the same man began his protest. "We just sort of went along with Jimmy here, who figured that this was the best way to dispose of them. They're breathing down his neck, and they do know something."

The girl's tone was scathing. "I'm sure that the Negotiating Committee is perfectly aware that there are tens of thousands of Jimmy Marriotts in their armies, who are against the withdrawal of Earth federation forces. And I'm equally sure they're not going to spend more than a minute or two on all the traitors put together."

Her analysis, Bray reflected, was astonishingly correct. But it didn't apply to Marriott. That such a highly trained man in such a minor position had sought contact with the leaders of the peace group among the Diamondians needed to be explained.

Far more important—he felt slightly awed—was that the girl was showing herself to be more of a power in all this than anyone had realized. She sounded like a leader.

But it had been equally urgent in Marriott's case to establish, as Bray had now done, that the officer was a collaborator.

He grew aware that Marriott himself was finally reacting, somewhat petulantly. "All right. All right. I give in. I'll sacrifice myself. I'll let this particular creature sleep it off in my office. But it's probably too late for Colonel Morton. He's already at the hospital, presumably still unconscious. And I can't stop the routine there once it's started. You'll agree it would look odd if one of our people suddenly tried to stop the forces that he had set in motion." He finished, "I'll hold Bray till morning as an insurance."

The girl seemed to accept the defeat, for after a pause, she said grudgingly, "I'm hoping that what you have done in setting such forces in motion on a person of Colonel Morton's stature doesn't make somebody suspicious. Pietro will go with

20

you, and in the morning he will make sure that Lieutenant Lester Bray does indeed leave your office a free man."

She broke off, sharply, "What keeps bothering me is, why didn't this young man take his superior officer to a hospital himself? How did you people make Morton unconscious?"

"How do you mean, we! We had nothing to do with it, my dear," said one of the familiar male voices.

The girl must have shaken her head, because her tone had a resigned note in it. "You people! You people amaze me. I took it for granted that Marriott arranged it. Now we have a complete mystery."

She was evidently walking back toward the house, because her voice was progressively farther away: "I'm going to have to speak to my father about applying methods for brain sharpening for some of you. How do we know that we haven't just witnessed another new Irsk technique?"

A door closed. The voice sound ended with a cut off effect.

A few moments later Marriott's car started.

For Bray, who had been unceremoniously dumped into the back seat, there was nothing to do but go along with the condition that he had created for himself.

On the way back to the military post at Corapo, he made the sounds of coming to, and by the time the car swung into the courtyard at the rear of the building, he was able to navigate by himself though barely.

"You'd better stay here tonight," said Captain Marriott, with apparent concern, as if he was giving his guest a choice.

Bray agreed. There were questions he wanted to ask which would sound better coming from a man who had slept off his liquor. And easier to ask if he didn't force any issues now.

Besides there was nothing he could do for Morton at this hour. The conspirators at whichever hospital Morton had been taken to would obviously impose barriers night or day. These would be especially effective at night.

So for him the day ended in a comfortable bed in the spare bedroom of Marriott's command apartment.

Three

IN THE MORNING when Bray entered the dining room, he noticed that the dark-haired man looked pale and had a distracted air about him.

"Anything wrong?" Bray asked politely, after they had exchanged good mornings.

He had a hopeful idea as to what Marriott's disturbance might consist of: opening the door of Bray's car the night before . . . consequences thereof.

"No, no." Marriott motioned vaguely. "Sit here, lieutenant."

Bray sat. There was silence as an Irsk waiter, who wore a green-striped waiter's coat served them breakfast. Several times Marriott seemed ready to speak. But they must have been thought movements only; no words came. Bray observed that the man was gazing off toward the wall behind him and took the opportunity to give his host a quick examination. He saw then that Marriott was unmistakably in shock.

Bray grew optimistic. There might be an opportunity here to make a bargain for Morton.

He began in a sober, neutral voice, "So those people last night were the Diamondian peace lovers?"

Momentarily that drew Marriott. He said, "Ordinary, well-meaning people of the kind that exist by the tens of millions on Diamondia."

After he had spoken he remained briefly animated. But, as the silence lengthened, the sick look came back into his eyes.

Bray had to shake his head over the meaning. He had not yet met an "ordinary" Diamondian.

"Who are these Irsk they're going to contact? Who do they represent?" Bray asked.

Once more, the visibly disturbed man who sat across from him came to a semblance of life. As Marriott explained it contact had been made with an Irsk group, the members of which professed to be Diamondian lovers. The group was prepared to launch powerful forces—it was said—against the unrelenting Diamondian haters among the Irsk.

The whole thing seemed farfetched to Bray.

"You really believe there is a Diamondian delegation out somewhere meeting an Irsk delegation?" Bray asked.

The incredulous tone of the question seemed finally to alert Marriott. "Of course, lieutenant"—his voice was sharp, condescending again—"these are very sincere, well-meaning people. The meeting, in fact, was to take place early this morning."

"Then it's done, and nothing went wrong with that delegation?"

"Well—" Marriott was suddenly uncertain. "There's something about Diamondians," he said finally, reluctantly, "that's different from other people. They're brilliant, they build the most beautiful things, write the most wonderful music, understand life and women and are exceptionally talented, but—"

"But what?"

"Nobody knows," said Marriott frankly.

There seemed to be nothing to say to that. The two men ate in silence, while Bray began to realize that he had a problem coming up soon. When he went out to his car and discovered that Morton's unconscious body was not there, what should his reaction be?

A bargain might be in order here. He began with determination. "Captain, you haven't seemed well this morning."

Marriott hesitated then braced himself, his expression suddenly that of a man who has come to a decision. "Lieutenant," he said, "there's something we should discuss. Your car—"

Bray recognized similarity of purpose and waited.

Marriott spoke firmly, "Last night, in the course of routinely observing the vehicles parked near this building, one of our men noticed that somebody had put what looked like a dead body into your car."

Bray wondered what kind of "routine" observation would have penetrated the almost opaque shadowing effect he had used to prevent observation of the interior of his machine. But he made no comment.

Marriott was continuing, "We actually patrol the entire town, but we particularly maintain a constant surveillance of all vehicles that come within a radius of two hundred yards of this building and use special devices to examine them.

Naturally, what we look for are concealed bombs and other deadly items that might destroy or damage our little structure here."

It did not seem unreasonable.

"We removed the body and sent it to a hospital," said Marriott.

"Who," asked Bray, "unlocked the door of the car?"

Marriott's dark gray gaze glowed directly into Bray's innocent blue eyes. He said tensely, "I did, lieutenant."

"Then you'll need to be demagnetized, captain."

"How do you mean?" The older man sounded puzzled. "I don't understand the term."

"I beg your pardon. It's an Intelligence term. Refers, sir, to a hypnotic alignment with another person." Bray pretended to give Marriott a searching examination, as if seeing certain details for the first time. "You show signs of the internal struggle, captain. You must have had a bad night."

Marriott's bright eyes glared at him, wide-eyed, waiting.

Bray explained the nature of the hypnotizing process, finished, "At the time there's a sense of confusion, and then progressively the other identity takes over."

Marriott nodded slowly. There was an uneasy expression on his face. "So it's that one," he said. "It requires the original hypnotizing mechanism to do the freeing."

Bray climbed to his feet. "While you write down," he said, "the name of the hospital to which you sent the body, I'll go and get the device and we'll release you."

A little later, Marriott did write a name down on a card. They parted outwardly on good terms, Bray saying, "I'd appreciate hearing if something came of the meeting. I can't quite believe private groups like this are going to solve the problem, but wish them luck. Goodbye and thanks."

He went out to a bright, sunny day and drove off in his car in the general direction of rescuing Morton, wherever he was. How that might be accomplished was distinctly unclear to Lieutenant Lester Bray. It was especially not clear after he discovered, as he had unhappily anticipated, that Morton was not at the hospital named on the card which Marriott had given him.

Where could he be? What condition was he in?

Four

WHAT COULD POSSIBLY happen to a Diamondian peace delegation out in the remote wilderness of an over-heated, steamy part of a continent on Diamondia VI?

Nobody lived in that particular segment of wilderness; not even Irsk. So by good reasoning, nothing could go wrong. The two peace delegations, the Diamondians and the Irsk, would meet and would arrive at an understanding. Since each delegation represented a substantial, responsible portion of their respective peoples, they would solve their problem without reference to the Negotiating Committee which had recently arrived from Earth.

That was the theory.

The main battle line stopped about a hundred miles farther north in the cooler mountains, where the Diamondians had cleverly created continuous provocations; so the fighting would be there . . . The Irsk never saw through stratagems of that kind.

And so—

In that certain Diamondia VI jungle called the Gyuma Ravine, the afternoon wore on. Beyond the ravine the sun hovered, less than four diameters above the highest peak of the hills to the west; and still it sank. To the group of Diamondians cautiously nearing the ravine, the world around them seemed to be coming more lifeless each passing moment, as if somehow its earlier strength was spent. And it needed a whole long night to prepare for day.

Illusion could not have been greater. The universe of jungle was not on the verge of sleep. It was waking up. The valley was already three-quarters alive.

The jungle accepted the coming of darkness almost too easily. Already, shadows were everywhere; and in some of the heavy growth areas, visibility was exceedingly dim. The thirty-foot stream that fed the most profuse of the growth was almost overwhelmed in places by the plant life it kept alive. Thousands of vines actually ventured into the running water and were only restrained from complete victory by the profusion of their own growth.

The stream survived here just as it had survived similar orgies of plant madness in a score of other valleys on its way down from the higher hills. It came in from the north across a narrow, grassy plain, gleaming at intervals as it followed its winding course through the sixteen-mile-long gauntlet of the ravine and then debouched by means of a steep-walled gorge into the reaches of another, hotter plain farther down.

The human peace delegation, approaching from the northeast, crept to the rim of the ravine on their knees. Their caution had nothing to do with their original purpose in being there in this remote area of the Diamondian-Irsk battle front.

Somebody had suggested, "Since our meeting isn't scheduled until tomorrow morning, why don't we do a little hunting?"

Everyone in the delegation was instantly aroused to excitement. A very good idea. A kind of expansive feeling went through the body of men. After all, we Diamondians had, long ago and at great expense, brought all these animals from Earth. What an excellent opportunity to gain a little return on the investment.

The presence of human beings had already jarred the environment in a curious fashion. A host of normal activities ceased to move forward in a straight line. Natural patterns began very subtly to transform, to break.

A rare, partly grown, marbled cat, little larger than a domestic tom, caught a whiff of man odor. And shrank back just as it was about to launch itself at an unsuspecting tree shrew.

The electric tension of the cat's muscles warned the shrew. It flicked under some rotting bark. Furious, the cat twisted off into the brush.

A quarter of a mile away, a pair of hardy hill panthers rose from the jungle grass, where they had spent the day. They stiffened as the alien scent, vaguer here, touched their alert nostrils. Their lips drew back in silent masks of snarls. They slunk off along the ravine until the loathsome odor troubled them no more.

It was not as easy as that for the ravine to get rid of the intelligent beings. There they were, smaller by weight and length than the lone crocodile that lurked two hundred yards downstream near a watering hole, hopelessly outmatched in every physical aspect by the great tiger that sometimes came from the lower jungles to hunt the stately sambur and wiry goral, and the elusive serow. Yet it was the men, not the animals, who dominated.

They lay, the eleven Diamondians, gun eased out now

26

across the lip of the valley pointing in the general direction of the target. Across the ravine, the two serow stood up. They had been lying in the shade during the heat of the day, but now they were hungry. For a few moments their black, goatian bodies silhouetted against the semiprecipice that was the opposite hillside. They stood there on a rocky ridge, perfect targets, their horned heads held high as they sniffed the air suspiciously.

During that span of moments eleven guns fired twelve times.

With anyone else it would be difficult to understand why every bullet missed. But a perfectly natural Diamondian sequence of events had taken place.

It had suddenly occurred to one man that he should be the one that actually killed a serow. So this man, a small, blond-haired, freckle-complexioned individual named Joaquin, as he lay there with his gun pointing across the ravine, watched the others out of the corners of his eyes; ignored the target.

Having all those sensitive Diamondian awarenesses, he detected instants in advance, that fingers were squeezing with the gentle skill of perfect markmanship.

He fired first. And missed because he was not looking at the target.

Every single other person present had, like the first man, been selected as a member of the peace delegation because he was, in addition to his other qualifications, a dead shot. But alas, they were all Diamondians. As they heard the first shot, automatic masculine jealousy surged through ten hearts. It was sufficient disturbance. Guns moved ever so slightly away from perfect alignments and fired off target.

At that point the individual who had caused the disaster hastily fired again.

The reason he missed his second shot was not because he was a Diamondian. There are other forces in the world, and one of these now dominated.

Since the Gyuma Ravine was not a part of the actual Diamondian-Irsk battle front, the rattle of gunfire impinged upon ten thousand ears that had never heard such a sound before. It was a thrilling staccato of noise. Its effect varied.

The two hill panthers, sturdy three year olds, heading along the ravine, looked back jumpily, then blinked and started to climb the hillside at their usual pace.

A dozen types of jungle cat, a pair of scaly anteaters, a common otter, a clawless otter, two ferret badgers, a hundred squirrels, some Indian mongooses, some hundreds of brilliantly colored birds, including several species of the prolific and variegated green pigeon, other pigeons, jungle fowl, silver and Kalij pheasants, and approximately a thousand other living creatures big enough to be aware of the outside world, and which made the ravine their home or base of operations, *paused* as that unnatural noise struck their ears. Paused tensely and then went about their business.

The two serow, of all the wild things in that ravine, reacted violently. The sound of the shots meant nothing. But the skittering zoom of the bullets striking the rocky ridge all around them, titillated every nerve in their bodies.

They uttered their cries of alarm; an explosive intermingling of snort and harsh whistle. And then they started to climb the precipice behind them. It was nearly a hundred feet to the top, but they were black streaks against the gray green brown wall of the hillside. In seconds, they were over the rim and out of sight.

Most of this reaction occurred in the time span between the two bullets fired by the little, blond-haired individual. *He* missed because the second time his target was already in motion.

Among the other ten men, several suspected at once what had happened. They were outraged. The rest were frustrated but uncertain.

Unfortunately for the human beings, the Irsk delegation had encamped behind some brush in an indentation only a few yards from where the serow had been at rest. Because of special Irsk abilities their presence did not disturb the two animals.

But the hail of Diamondian bullets disturbed the Irsk.

A typical deadly Diamondian-Irsk madness now took place. The angry among the Diamondians turned on each other, seeking the culprit with loud, passionate accusations. Swiftly, the others realized what had happened. Utterly oblivious of where they were, their yelling voices created a bedlam that sounded like a numerous body of men. Then one Diamondian realized the danger and began the difficult task of shushing down his excited companions. He was too late. The sound of so many voices decided the momentarily hesitant Irsk. Acting in what they believed was self-defense, they lobbed a hand variation of the Duald weapon into the exact center of the Diamondian peace delegation.

Energy flowed from it in all directions. It was an energy with an impact potential. As if thousands of bits of metal moved from it in straight lines.

28

One or more of those bits discharged in the space occupied by every human except the one who had caused the trouble in the first place. Before each irresistible impact, death was instantaneous. During the flow, Joaquin happened to be bending down behind a massive rock for no reason but one that God would know.

Hearing the energy discharge, he bent even closer to the ground and waited there for the hissing sound of the energy to cease.

When it had done so, he departed without a backward glance.

Five

HUMAN BEINGS afoot, aknee, or astomach in a jungle require measurable time to move from point A to point B. For an untimed period following the shots, the jungle lay silent.

To the west the sun sank visibly lower. A breeze, which had been on its way for some time, reached the ravine and whisked along it in little gusts that swayed branches and rustled leaves. It also brought a cool breath of air to the fetidly hot valley.

The lone survivor of the Diamondian peace delegation, Joaquin, attained the shelter of a clump of vinelike trees. Crouched tensely in that shielding tangle, rifle ready, he watched the uneven line of hill that stretched to the right and to the left a hundred feet above him.

His situation was desperate. Although at first he had believed himself unscathed, he had presently discovered a soggy red area high up on the back of his shirt. A shoulder muscle had been cut by a flying object. It bled profusely.

And night was falling.

Wounded, he was of the jungle. The realization was slow to penetrate, for all his strength and all his will were taken up with the labor of moving his body inch by inch through the night and the undergrowth.

For a long time he was not even conscious of where he was going. There was only the blackness and his movement and the vague life within him, struggling to manifest itself.

He tired at last. He lay motionless in the grass, the sound of his own breathing loud in his ears. And it was then that the thought came that he was now subject to the whims of the wilderness.

Understanding also penetrated of where he was going: the stream. He had to have water. The need was beyond all reasoning. His mouth was dry, his tongue moistureless, his body drained.

Lying there, he must have fainted . . . He woke with a start. He must have been unconscious for a long period, because a moon rode the eastern sky where there had been only stars before—and the hot, odorous breath of an animal was blowing gustily in his face. Two eyes glared yellowly at him from a head that was briefly shapeless.

Joaquin shrank, then jerked his arm up and out. His hand struck a bony head painfully.

"Get away!" he yelled.

It was not a very hard blow and not a very loud yell, but the eyes retreated hungrily. And now that it was not so near, Joaquin saw that the creature was a jackal.

He rasped at it, "So you were trying to get up your nerve to sink your teeth into my neck. Beat it!"

In spite of his instant rage, he felt relief that the danger was no greater. He shoved his half-drawn revolver back into its holster and looked around him. And saw a second jackal, probably the mate of the first one, sitting on its haunches, staring at him.

The sight of the second creature shocked him. He dared not faint again.

Stronger, more desperate than before, was the realization that he had lost blood. And that he would be a dead man unless he got water.

He forced himself to his knees, and began to crawl. The moon withdrew beyond the overhanging foliage. And moved up half an hour in the sky while he groped forward. At the end of that time, he suddenly heard the mumbling of the water in the blackness ahead.

Frantic, he tried to push on. And couldn't. Only an elephant or a tank could have broken through the mass of creepers around the creek's bed, and only a tank would have tried it. Joaquin turned wearily downstream.

He came abruptly upon the bare-banked pool of the crocodile. The mud at the edge was cool and soothing to his fevered hands. He splashed as he drank, and some of his blood drifted out and down to the log lying half in the mud, half in the water, twenty feet away.

The log stirred and launched itself with scarcely a ripple.

30

In the moonlight, its eyes glowed like small saucers; and Joaquin, resting from the labor of drinking, watched them with an interest so dim that it took an effort to think wonderingly:

A crocodile! I'd better shoot it!

Again, that strong rage. He aimed at one of the eyes. He had no sense of being personally involved until the crash of the gun awoke a dozen echoes in the valley and jarred him out of his daze.

He stared, startled, as the water whitened with the churnings of a heavy body. It didn't need any effort of will to move away from that nightmare animal. It needed only the effort.

The camp and safety seemed a very, very, long way off.

For a while, the jungle left him alone. He lived, moved and had his being on an animal trail that tunneled endlessly through a night lighted only by a lacework of foliage-filtered moonbeams.

But he was more aware, and with a return of intelligence came also the conviction that he must reach the peace delegation's main camp before they, also, were ambushed.

With that awareness of purpose came his first real fear that the jungle might prevent him from carrying it out. A few hours before he had been immune, beyond all the threats and all the dangers. But now the Irsk had chopped his short, strong body down to the level of the jungle.

He crouched, shrinking, as a shadow slipped across the moon. Almost instantly he saw that it was a cloud. But the spasm of fright had struck. The jungle was suddenly alive. It whispered and sighed. It rustled, it hissed and it creaked. It made padding noises, like footfalls coming near then retreating.

He was lying there almost blank when he became aware that somebody was standing a few feet off to one side, staring at him. His first impression was that it was an Irsk. But as Joaquin raised his head and glared at the thing, almost petrified with fear, he realized that it was a luminous shape, and that he could see through it.

A fearful memory came to Joaquin. Stories he had heard that every twilight Irsk demons and ghosts flew down from the upper air and shook branches, made noises in water, strode through the underbrush and uttered moans and indescribable cries.

This transparent being came toward him silently, bent over him and said something. Joaquin, a good Catholic, instantly

31

recognized that he was being subjected to a wile of the devil; and he mentally closed his ears, determined that not a single meaning would be allowed inside his head. Yet he presently grew aware that he was being asked to promise something. In view of his weakened condition, he stated faithfully that he would do as the ghost wished, but naturally absolved himself from having to do so.

The sound of his loud voice replying, and also very possibly the shining movement of the thing, stampeded three wild pigs that had been rooting ten feet away. They broke out onto the trail, and Joaquin had to scramble to avoid them. As it was, the hooves of one of them cut his right leg as it charged past. By the time he was able to look around, the luminous shape had disappeared.

Oblivious of the keen pain, he staggered to his feet and began to run. After a hundred yards he was teetering along at a crazy walk, and a little farther on he fell to the ground, too weak to move.

His brain, drained of physical support, was even weaker than his body. A small-toothed palm civet yowled somewhere in the near jungle. Joaquin shouted at it.

That was the way he spent the next hour, crawling forward like a mindless automaton and shouting loudly at every sound the jungle made.

There weren't many sounds. The lesser beings of the jungle do not advertise their presence. And the rest avoided the noisy demon in amazed alarm.

The patrol from the peace delegation's entourage found him a hundred yards from camp just after he had fired his fifth bullet at an enormous leaf swaying in a gentle breeze a few feet in front of him.

Of the numerous sins of Joaquin on that day and that night, not the least, then, was his decision to say nothing of the visitation from the devil out there in the darkness of the jungle. He was given water and food and effective medical attention, that within an hour restored him enormously. As soon as he was able, he told his false tale of Irsk betrayal, which by now he believed implicitly.

Meanwhile, the Irsk delegation had, of course, reported to *their* backup army that *they* had been ambushed . . . and so it was already late indeed for good sense.

Naturally the Diamondian peace backup group sent an urgent request for reinforcements. General Philippe Ferraris, sitting back in his headquarters, was shocked since the peace plan was his daughter's pet idea. But he dutifully dispatched

32

a thousand paratroopers as an intermediate force. These men descended on the ravine shortly after dawn. They found already entrenched a powerful Irsk force, that had come quickly and quietly during the night, anticipating further human—the way they thought of it—shenanigans.

By nine o'clock, the battle had attained a state of fiery sincerity. Death, according to reports, was everywhere. And the Diamondian general had discreetly decided to await its outcome before communicating the disaster to his daughter.

All this, while for Morton the previous afternoon there had been—

Six

DISTANCE AND BLACKNESS!

Stars . . . familiar formations. Morton recognized that he was looking at the stellar configurations in, around, and including Diamondia.

Looking at them—he was vaguely startled to realize—from over a thousand miles out in space.

Even as he gazed in developing astonishment, he had a peculiar, uneasy feeling that there was a threat nearby him which he should see.

He tried to turn and . . . just like that he was walking along a street beside two roughly dressed Irsk.

And there was a mild thought in his mind that he was not going to allow himself to be involved in any foolishness.

No, you cannot have the Lositeen Weapon.

Morton realized, in what seemed a perfectly natural fashion, that the two Irsk nationalists were trying to persuade him to give to the rebel armies what they called the "darkness destroying force."

As they glided along beside him, gesticulating with subtly meaningful movements of their tentacles, they argued heatedly against his point of view.

Their point: It was shameful for an Irsk to be human-oriented. One of these days, all Diamondian-loving Irsk would be declared enemies of the planet.

"And if that happened, Lositeen, you'd be on the list of traitors."

Once such a decision was made, it would be death for every green-striped Irsk on Diamondia.

"So think now, Lositeen, do you really want to have your Irsk brothers against you on that not too far off day—within hours after the federation forces leave?"

Morton smiled and again shook his head at the two. "Don't bother me, gentlemen," he said. "It is very brave of you to come in from the hills. But you should really be more discreet for the sake of your families, who would be devastated if anything happened to their favorite sons."

The word "families" seemed unusually important, for his attention went back to it.

Then he was standing on the street, gazing after the two Irsk. The way they walked off, the impatience of their manners, telegraphed rage and frustration. Morton found himself smiling at their intensity. As he resumed his own walking, it seemed to him that there was something that they didn't understand that he did. It was something that he had solved for himself; and they didn't even grasp that it was a problem.

He was about to review what his special understanding was when, abruptly, the truth of what was occurring penetrated to Morton.

What's happening? Where am I?

He tried, then, to stop. And tried to look around. But he couldn't stop. Nor could he turn his head.

Under him, his body continued to stride along the street of what Morton now saw was a little town. The place seemed familiar.

Must be one of two hundred little Diamondian communities he had visited since the take-over.

But where?

How had he got here?

For God's sake, I'm sitting in that car with Lieutenant Bray. How can I be—elsewhere?

Who is this? It's not me.

My God, it's not me!

The numbed feeling that came had no counterpart in his experience. Yet, all the while, even as he had these terrifying feelings . . . under him, around him, and through him, the body of—what had the Irsk called him? Lositeen, walked on, unaffected, apparently unaware of any observer.

He thought automatically: *My name is Charles Morton, not Lositeen . . .*

It seemed as if he had to make that defense.

Once more, he tried to force the body to stop. But Lositeen

continued alternately to put out, first, a right tentacle, then a left, and so on, each time stiffening it so that the muscles in it took on some of the rigidity of bone. In this rigid state the tentacles supported him as easily as legs held up a human being.

Morton finally gave up his spasmodic attempts to control the body of an Irsk and watched helplessly as Lositeen walked on and presently entered a hardware store. He went straight to a back room, hung up his green-striped coat, put on a green-striped smock, came out and went behind the counter.

He began to serve customers, Diamondian farmer types mostly.

Surely, at any second, this crazy thing will end as quickly as it started.

But the minutes became an hour, and the hour lengthened into half an afternoon. Morton noticed a development tendency on his part to go alone in a rhythmic way with whatever Lositeen did or said.

As if I'm saying it or doing it.

It seemed a dangerous tendency, and he resisted it.

By late afternoon his thought went back to the conversation the two Irsk nationalists had had with Lositeen about the ancestral weapon.

That's all we need in this murderous war, another weapon, one more powerful than any to date.

Incredibly, the weapon was in the possession of a human-oriented Irsk who was a hardware store clerk in a little town somewhere in man-inhabited Diamondia—that was the big continent, the one with the temperate climate. So Morton had been told, when he was still en route.

. . . Until he found out the sadly bitter truth:

On Diamondia, temperate meant a hundred in the shade.

Six o'clock came. Closing time.

The mild-mannered, young Irsk took off his smock. Next he put on his coat, said goodbye to the two other green-striped Irsk clerks and to the voluble Diamondian owner of the store and went outside. He walked along the street, substantially retracing the route that had brought him to the store at what—it was retrospectively apparent—had been the lunch hour.

The Diamondian sun, as brilliant as a blue white diamond, was sinking behind the western hills, and there were long shadows everywhere. Lositeen walked on, arriving presently in the Irsk quarter at the town's outskirts.

As he saw the ancient ruins all around, Morton was electrified. His civilian training was architect, and he had been eager to look into this old, old civilization. Until now, impossible. Too many things to do.

Dazzled and expectant, he realized that Lositeen's destination was the biggest house in the very center of the Irsk community.

Unfortunately, the approach to the structure was a familiar one to Lositeen, and he scarcely glanced at it. Indeed, he actually turned his head away from key areas. So Morton was unable to look at the repair work that had been done on the—for want of a better term—plastic.

One of these days, he thought, it will be interesting to discover how that hard material ever broke, and what they did to fix it.

Just like that his own desperate situation was momentarily gone from his mind. He waited in delighted expectation of seeing the delicately wrought interior, hitherto available to him only in photographs and picture magazines; not the same as the real thing in its own setting.

Morton anticipated first the front hall. Then other supremely beautiful interior views.

That thought ended.

Hey, where is he going?

Disappointingly, instead of using the front entrance Lositeen was following a pathway through weeds to the rear of the fairylike building. He entered a small room which had a gracefully curving ceiling, yes; that was shaped usefully so that odors could escape through a natural flue in the ceiling, interesting; that was neatly filled with a type of automatic machine, which the disappointed humans had discovered worked only in the house into which they were built (concealed in the walls), good; and which, except where there had been some precolonist disaster, could not be removed—fine.

The kitchen! Or, at least, what had been converted for that purpose.

Morton resigned, was prepared to be interested even in it. But Lositeen took his surroundings for granted and scarcely glanced around. He touched a wall. It opened; and he removed a plate of, of all things, pizza. He thereupon seated himself at a table and ate absently, mostly staring down at the table. Morton grew aware that darkness was shading the translucent walls.

Abruptly, that brought him back with a start to his own condition.

Soon it will be time to go to bed. To sleep.

What then? Will I sleep, also?

There was a sound at one of the doors that led from the kitchen to the rest of the house. As Lositeen turned, an Irsk girl came in.

Lositeen stood up with quick courtesy, and said, "A beautiful evening to you, Ajanttsa."

The young Irsk woman brushed aside his words. She said curtly, "Did the fighters talk to you?"

"Oh—they came here?" Lositeen sounded surprised, and then he became uneasy. "Ajanttsa, you and your father must be careful not to become involved with these dangerous dyl. The Diamondians show no mercy in such matters; you know that."

The girl hesitated. She stood there, then, and since Lositeen was gazing directly at her, Morton was able to observe her clearly. In his brief weeks on Diamondia, he had made intense efforts to learn something of the Irsk.

And so he was able to evaluate that, by Irsk male standards, Ajanttsa was an especially beautiful female of the species. Her lips were thinner, her eyes slightly larger—and greenish, not blue. The long, thin head and the extra lean, tapering body, with its slender, delicate arm and leg tentacles, gave her an unusual elegance of appearance.

Yet he realized that Lositeen, for a reason that was not clear, was not particularly conscious of or interested in these delectable qualities, much to Ajanttsa's irritation.

She'd been placed here, Morton thought shrewdly, to stir up this fellow. An amazing but simple plot on the part of the anti-Diamondian Irsk to involve the possessor of the Lositeen Weapon.

Ajanttsa spoke, "You were not affected by their arguments?"

At her question, Lositeen simply smiled.

"My dear Ajanttsa," he said, "I belong to that large group of Irsk who intend to help reestablish law and order on Diamondia. By that I mean human law. Irsk being almost entirely Diamondian human conditioned and so overemotional, this is not an easy task. As witness you, my dear, for even as you fight the Diamondians, you use their language. And also notice that you eat their food instead of using the energy method of sustenance by which we Irsk maintained ourselves before the coming of these human beings. I want you to

37

witness, too, what has just happened at the Gyuma Ravine. I have mentally protested our delegation's hasty reaction in that situation. There has to be another explanation for what happened there. But my protest is just one tiny drop of reason in an ocean of temporary insanity. It's difficult to know what will now happen, but it doesn't look promising."

"Good," said the girl.

Whereupon she turned, went back out the door and closed it behind her.

When she had gone, Lositeen took the dish from which he had been eating and slipped it into a slot in the wall. Then he went through a second door. This one led to a vaguely lighted, large hallway. It was so dark that of all the beauty that must have been there, Morton could see only streaks of silver. He had an impression of a winding staircase that was held in place by almost invisible threads of some shining material.

It was toward this stairway that Lositeen made his way.

He paused at the foot of the staircase.

His head turned. His eyes gazed at a large closed door, which was off to his left, opposite from the kitchen. The door was dimly visible in that darkness, a different shape from the wall on either side rather than something that was definitely identifiable.

Lositeen's thought was: *Should I look in there? Make sure all is well with—*

With what? It wasn't clear. Morton was unable to grasp the thought.

Whatever it was seemed important to Lositeen. Yet in the end he rejected the impulse and, reaching, grasped the stair railing.

Morton anticipated that he would walk up.

He didn't.

He was up.

Morton thought: *For God's sake!*

He realized that the transition had been virtually instantaneous. The finely divided hand tentacle of Lositeen touched the railing; and he was up.

And there was no time to think about it. Lositeen walked past several deeper shadows that looked like doors, and finally entered a small room at the rear of a side hallway.

In the room, dimly visible, were a bed, a chair, a tiny bureau and a carpet on the floor. It was, to the extent that Morton could make it out, Earth style furniture. Lositeen undressed in the dark. And, when he had crawled under the

38

sheets, he lay for a while in the shadows, smiling in an unconcerned way.

At least Morton, detected that it was the enigmatic Irsk grimace on the face; and the feeling was one of relaxed good nature.

Lying there, Lositeen thought: *"What's wrong with being a Diamondian? One has to be something, and they are the first artistic race to come along.*

His smile faded. His face muscles grew tight. He spoke aloud finally, softly, and addressed—somebody:

"It is a grave error to have done what you did and to continue to do it. Again, today, I have been approached by the rebel Irsk, asking me for the Lositeen Weapon. Are they making this request on your behalf? Since you already control the darkness, I wouldn't be surprised if you are pressuring them to hand my ancestral weapon over to you. It is true that it can be used to supplement the darkness, but it's real purpose is to protect the Irsk nation if an emergency were to arise. I have one question: what can you really gain, you who have such a short life span? There seems no point in so much ambition."

Having spoken, Lositeen waited. Finally, he said: "What? Not even the courtesy of a reply! Very well, if that is your answer, then I shall extend my communication-by-duplicate barrier to you, also. Goodbye."

Whereupon Lositeen turned over and peacefully went to sleep.

Morton woke up in a hospital room.

Seven

Colonel Charles Morton found his uniform behind some sliding doors. The weapons concealed in it had been removed from all the little hidden places. Which was too bad but to be expected. Presumably they were locked away somewhere with his other personal effects.

But at least his clothes were available.

He was at the window by the time he had that realization, awkwardly manipulating the old-fashioned blind . . . These damned New Naples people, with their crazy idea of re-creating old Naples right down to the inconveniences.

Abruptly, the blind zoomed up to the window top, arriving there with a cracking sound as loud as a pistol shot. Morton winced but swiftly forgot that as he gazed out of the window and saw that he was looking toward the east.

The Diamondian sun was visible high above the ancient buildings that he could see from the hospital bedroom. As he surveyed the scene below and before him, Morton estimated that he was on the upper floor of the hospital and that the sun was about three hours above the rooftops.

So in New Naples it was nine o'clock in the morning.

It's got to be the next morning, he told himself anxiously. There was no point in the time elapsed being longer than that.

What disturbed him was that there had to be a sequence of events that had brought his body here to this bed. From Lieutenant Bray's car one day to the hospital here the next morning was a long time. During that time who had got to him, and what had they discovered?

As these uneasy thoughts poured through his mind, Morton headed for the phone that he now discovered beside the bed. The switchboard had evidently not been barred to this room; for it gave him an outside line. He called his office and found himself talking to Technical Sergeant Struthers, his secretary. "Listen," commanded Morton, "here's what I want you to do. Bring my station wagon, and come to the—" he paused to read the fine print on the phone "—the Hospital of the Incuribili, the rear entrance.

Struthers promised, and Morton hung up, greatly encouraged. Still, it wasn't going to be easy.

With that intense thought driving him, he grabbed again for the phone. A few moments later, his rank having got him past a secretary and nurse, he was explaining to Andrew Gerhardt, M.D. psychiatrist, telling him truthfully what had happened to him and requesting an appointment for 1:30 that afternoon.

Morton concluded earnestly, "I'm sure, doctor, that this matter is in your province, and that it would be unwise for doctors here in the hospital to prescribe for it."

Dr. Gerhardt's youthful voice held in it exactly the note of asperity that Morton had hoped to evoke, as he assured Morton that, indeed, his problem seemed to be nonfunctional. "And if you have any difficulties, colonel, you may certainly use me as a reference."

Morton hung up from that call feeling considerably more cheerful, though how he would handle Gerhardt later was another matter. As he shaved, he realized something else. From the moment of his awakening, he had waited in an unpleasant expectation for each period of blackness. And every time that the blackness had threatened to engulf his brain, he had the shocked conviction that he would again be . . . transported.

That fear was gone. More than twenty minutes had gone by, and the blackness had come four times and had gone again. And still he was himself.

Even as he had the realization, the darkness surged once more. He paused for it to go by and, when it had done so, was amazed anew at human beings. *How easily we accustom ourselves to fantasia, to madness.*

He was fully dressed now. He paused to put on his military cap, and he was standing there adjusting it for an authoritative effect when the phone rang.

It was Lieutenant Bray, breathless and apologetic. What Morton presently abstracted from the young officer's flustered dialogue was that Bray had come with Struthers; and they were now at the downstairs back entrance, waiting to whisk Morton away from the hospital.

As the import of Bray's words penetrated, Morton was electrified. "Hey," he said, "maybe this will work out."

It was a type of escape problem that had always interested him in his idle moments. And so now fascinated, he headed for the door of the room.

Instants later, he stepped forth and was in the corridor.

The hallway outside his door was bright, gleaming, clean—lit up by a long line of ceiling lights. About one dozen persons were visible along its eighth of a mile of doors and carpeting and painted yellow walls; and a mere three others emerged from separate doors, as Morton strode at even but rapid pace toward what seemed to be the way out.

Were any of those people keeping an eye on him? —It was impossible to tell. But he was not happy when two of the original dozen—both men—were the only persons who walked into the elevator with him.

Morton stepped politely to the rear of the machine and stood with his back to the wall. The men seemed to be unconnected with each other; for they stood pensive, separate. Both were blond, burly Diamondians and presumably had been visiting patients. Which was odd at this hour in the morning. Hospital visitors—as Morton recalled uneasily—were afternoon and evening phenomena.

He had already glanced at the light numbering system

41

above the door; and that told him that his floor was number twelve—the top. (So his earlier guess about that was correct.)

The machine started down and stopped at floor eight. As the door glided open, it revealed a man with an unoccupied wheelchair. As he pushed this gingerly into the elevator, the two Diamondians and Morton got out of the way and were pressed into closer proximity off to one side.

The attendant with the chair was a rather fine-looking man in his late thirties with a decisive air about him. After he had made certain that his vehicle was properly inside the confined space, and after the door had closed and the elevator was again heading down, he said quietly, "Let's tighten the rhythm, friends."

The words had the fateful sound of a signal; and, since it was three against one, Morton said quickly, "I surrender."

Did he? Would he? He wasn't sure.

He waited, not yet decided as to how he would react.

The handsome young man produced a syringe. "Sit down in this wheelchair, colonel, and accept this medicine peacefully."

Was this murder? Morton doubted it. It wasn't necessary for these people to kill him, and no one seemed to be in a great passion. So *that* wasn't it, either.

Without a word, Morton sat down, pulled up his sleeve and watched as the man methodically sterilized the skin and then inserted the needle and pushed.

The task completed, the doctor (which, presumably, he was) straightened, and said, "Colonel, the first reaction of the drug I have injected is that you cannot speak or move. Next, you will doze and become unconscious for about eight hours. At that time, someone will ask you some questions. I strongly urge that you answer them correctly."

It was all pretty ridiculous, but deadly. He was able to deduce, sadly, that his phone calls out of his room must have been monitored. So really he had had no chance at all to get away.

The elevator stopped. The door opened. One of the two men rolled the wheelchair out into what proved to be a sort of side entrance. As he saw that, Morton had his first rueful realization about the location of his room. He had been in a wing of the hospital from which he couldn't easily reach the main lobby or even the main building at the rear of which Bray and Struthers would be waiting.

The men were treating the situation like a patient discharge. "Thank you, doctor," one said to the third man. The "doctor" said casually, "I'll accompany you out to your car."

Which he did. In the course of the short journey that now ensued, several people walked by, including two nurses. But they seemed to accept what they saw. And then there was the parking lot and the station wagon.

The two strong men lifted the wheelchair with Morton in it into the rear of the car. One got in beside him. The other took the driver's seat. They waved goodbye to the doctor, who waved back and then waited until the machine turned through a high gateway and into a narrow street.

Seconds later they were driving along a winding alleyway of New Naples. Which was the last outside visualization that Morton remembered afterward.

At that point, his body sagged into its second unconsciousness state in less than twenty-four hours.

Eight

THE SPEEDING STATION WAGON moved rapidly along the alleyway but soon emerged onto a wider thoroughfare. The two Diamondians hummed a little as they and their captive jetted along. They were both happy with their achievement.

"Isolina will be pleased," said the driver, glancing back at his companion and for several seconds trusting the safety of the machine and its passengers to his guardian angel, who apparently was looking the other way also. Because when he again faced forward, he had two choices. Instant death if he continued the way he was going. Or take the chance of jumping into a space in the next lane, a space that to anyone else measured about four feet. But he obviously saw it as twenty feet and swerved into it with that conviction firmly fixed into his mind. In that lane brakes squealed for a quarter of a mile back; and then there, magically, was the space provided for him by God.

It was morning, and the sky was steel blue; the air already hot, with the promise of hell only an hour or so away. They came to a wide, modern thoroughfare. The driver swung their vehicle onto it at the exact, tire-screaming speed of the score of other machines that took the turn before them, beside them and just behind. The sound that was momentarily created did not precisely tear the heavens apart, but it was an attempt in that direction.

The man at the wheel wrinkled his nose at the acrid odor of burning rubber. And he was about to settle down to a steady, high-speed, bumper to bumper transport when the man in the rear said tensely, "George, we are being followed."

"By whom, Pietro?"

Several car loads of those blasted Irsk, dressed in the striped clothes of the Friends of the Diamondian People."

The station wagon speeded up by jumping to the second lane from the left. "Did they follow, Pietro?" asked the driver, without turning.

"Yes."

"Don't worry," said the man at the wheel, "I will give those people the slip."

A minute after that he had made it to a side street with such fine timing that the three cars which carried the Irsk were unable to swerve after him, and so they zoomed on past the intersection. George raced up the side street, turned right at the first corner, then right again at the next one, and so back to the wide thoroughfare from which he had escaped a minute before. He now resumed his breakneck speed, and in another little while they came to the botanical gardens which Morton, had he been conscious, would have recognized as just about where Bray and he had been the previous afternoon.

At this point, the driver guided the hurtling car into another side street, then left into a second one, and into a narrow alleyway from which he abruptly spun the vehicle through a gate that led to a spacious courtyard at the rear of a large, three-story house.

Morton's two captors tumbled hastily out of the car. The one with Morton jumped down and the other catapulted out of the front seat and charged around to the back. Almost effortlessly they lifted Morton down to the cobbled stone and, without pausing, began to wheel him toward the house.

The rear entrance was through an ornamental door on the ground floor, but by climbing a concrete embankment to the right it was possible to reach a screen door that opened into the second story.

It was to this second-story that Morton was hauled. The effort of moving a limp body and the chair it was in up the embankment was almost too much for the two men. They puffed and wheezed and took time off to regain their strength—but they made it. George knocked on the door.

There was a pause, then the sound of footsteps, and then a young woman, neatly dressed and wearing a tiny, green hat, came and stared questioningly at the trio through the screen.

She spoke in a rich, pleasant, contralto voice, "Bring him in here."

Having uttered the words, she opened the door and held it while the wheelchair was pushed through. Inside was dimness, high ceilings and even a sense of coolness.

They came to a door which the young woman opened. "In here," she said.

"Here," turned out to be a woman's bedroom. The woman said, "Lay him on the bed facing the window."

Isolina Ferraris watched the two burly young men from narrowed eyes as they turned to go out. She had a timeless suspicion of Diamondian males; and so now she said, "Anything go wrong?"

"Nope." That was George.

Pietro, who parted his lips presumably to say the same thing, closed them and nodded.

"Everything worked out all right? No problems?"

"Perfect," said George of the innocent face.

When they had gone out, when the two men were in the courtyard again, Pietro said uneasily, "Shouldn't you have told her about the Irsk following us?"

The other man was scathing. "You don't tell things like that to a woman. We gave them the slip, didn't we?"

He walked off without waiting for a reply. His attitude reflected disgust with the stupidity and unmanliness of a male who didn't understand reality.

Up in the bedroom, the woman walked over and looked down at the unconscious man. She shook her head finally, with a faint satirical smile, and then said aloud, "Diamondia is not the safest place in the world for a member of the Negotiating Committee, is it, colonel? Unconscious twice within twenty-four hours. Still," she frowned, "that first time bothers me. How did that happen? It would have been foolish of us to let you be taken off the planet before we'd learned something about *that*."

She turned and walked to the door. "I shall be back this evening—and you had better have some good answers."

She opened the door and went out.

Seven hours ticked by on the pretty clock on the dresser.

During their slow progression, the heat of the Diamondia day moved into the room. Great beads of sweat broke out on the face of the man on the bed, but he did not stir nor show signs of returning consciousness until evening.

... A sense of brightness—that was Morton's initial awareness. For a long time that was all; but he realized that he was thinking or, rather, capable of thinking. Somewhere in there the numbness began to lift. First, his body tingled and tingled. Slowly the return of feeling spread along his limbs. And suddenly, he was able to open his eyes.

For the first time, he grew aware that he was lying on his side facing a window.

He had a strictly limited view of a tree just outside the window; and inside—a part of a room, an embroidery that hung on the wall beside the window, and a chair with a book lying on it, standing in the near corner under a floor lamp.

Maybe in about a minute, he thought, I can turn and see the rest of the room, including the door. And then—

He was having the vaguely hopeful thought that he would even recover the use of his limbs completely before anybody came ... when behind him the door opened and somebody entered.

Morton tried to turn and couldn't. There *was* muscular response but no strength. After a moment he accepted the defeat—and waited.

A pause. Then a woman's rather sweet voice said, "I am Isolina Ferraris. I want to discuss your unconsciousness of yesterday."

She completed the thought in a sterner tone, "We must know how that happened, sir—can you speak?"

Morton parted his lips, and to his surprise the word "Yes!" sort of burst forth.

Encouraged by that success, he tried once more to move, to turn. Nothing occurred.

But inwardly, he braced himself—for truth.

For the people of Diamondia, it was, so to say, a quarter of midnight. And there was no time to be devious. He had intended the previous afternoon to try to convince this young woman to give him straight answers about the peace delegation. And straightforwardness still seemed like a good thought. The question of whether or not she would believe his fantastic story was at issue.

Aloud he said, "I'll be glad to tell you exactly what happened to me—except there's a name I won't give, at least not until I feel more trust in you—"

46

He told her his experience. He withheld the name of Lositeen. He didn't know the name of the village.

When he had finished, there was a long pause. It was impossible even to surmise what her expression was. All he had to go by was a voice from somewhere behind him; and that voice was silent. He did wonder what a Diamondian might think of his fantastic account.

He couldn't imagine.

He wondered aloud, tentatively. "Has anyone—any scientist—ever suggested that the physics of the space around this planet is different?"

That elicited a reply. "It's only a kind of energy machine," the woman said, "so that at least is a relief."

It was one of those statements to which there was no obvious response. In those words she made nothing of a device which could render a man unconscious at a distance and transfer his awareness (self) into the mind of another being. If his perception was correct, it was actually an energy field so vast that it literally enveloped an entire planet. Contemplating that, *he* felt no relief.

He said, "A machine like that would have a colossal maintenance problem. I wouldn't be surprised if the finite logic number was above a hundred, which is fantastic."

Isolina wanted to know what finite logic was.

Morton shook his head. It was not the moment for a lecture on the history of the development of logic. So all he said was, "It's a term that has to do with the difference between a mathematical logic system and the facts of nature. In mathematics they have the concept of the "set": a collection of similar objects which are mathematically treated as duplicates. In nature there are no duplicates. The difference beween members of a set is best illustrated by conceiving of a set of Diamondians."

Isolina said with a shudder that she could see what he meant.

Morton concluded his analysis rather grimly. "It boils down to what instructions was that machine out there given? What must it do if breakdown threatens?"

The young woman was silent. So Morton said. "What that Irsk—in whose mind I was—said to his girl friend about a disaster to the peace delegation at the Gyuma Ravine—what about that?"

"I will call my father," Isolina said drably. She added, as if a thought had come. "It doesn't make complete sense. That meeting was not supposed to take place until early this morn-

47

ing, and yet your Irsk spoke of it as having happened yesterday."

For that Morton had no explanation.

Another pause. Then the woman's voice went on, defiantly, "I think I had better come to my special relation to all this. I am a woman, colonel, who tries to enlist the support of leading males in the Earth federation forces. I started close to the bottom with men like—well, never mind. But now I'm getting near the top, and this is where you come in."

As she spoke, she came around the bed and stood between Morton and the window; stared down at him. Morton had seen several photographs of her, so there was no question. Here, indeed, was Isolina Ferraris.

A faint, cynical smile was on that patrician face. "Colonel," she said, "what is your view of a woman who sleeps with a dozen men every month?"

Morton gazed up without criticism into eyes that dared him to be critical. Since he was not involved with her, not committed, he could notice that in the flesh she was a superior beauty—better looking than her pictures. Her features were even, her eyes blue and flashing, her skin very white. There was perhaps a little too much emotion in the eyes. The face was slightly flushed, somehow implying a buried shame. But it was a determined face. Here was a young woman with a beautiful body and a beautiful face, who intended to use those qualities for victory and survival.

He said, in a conciliatory voice, "Knowing that a woman's desire is for true love, I find myself regretting that circumstances have denied you that outcome. However," he continued, "I'm also reminded of a friend of mine, who observed a plain woman and a beautiful woman, both of whom are making the same compromise here on Diamondia as you are. For some reason he expressed concern about the future of the beautiful woman, but none about the future of the plain one. My feeling was that the plain one also craved love, nurtured the hope that someday it would be available to her."

The young woman was frowning. Her eyes studied him, puzzled. "What is the point of that comparison?" she asked.

"Since you are beautiful, I notice in myself the same greater concern for your future, which is unfair to that plain woman. So I realize I am no better than my friend."

She laughed. "Oh!" She added quickly, "I have discovered that men may be concerned about my future, but they don't hesitate to contribute to my downfall. What I am trying to say is that as soon as you are able to function physically with your whole body—which should be in two or three hours—I shall crawl into bed there with you and hope that, in consequence, this will cause you to be a friend of the Diamondian people."

Morton said nothing. He felt quite blank.

The young woman was speaking again. "Why don't you try to sleep? Perhaps, when you awaken, it will be to a pleasant surprise."

Morton said, "I'll have to get to the bathroom. I can feel the pressure building."

"Hmmm." She frowned. "I'll send George up with some kind of bedpan."

"Good," said Morton. "And tell him to hurry."

"He can also help you get undressed," she said.

And she went out.

Nine

MORTON CAME TO peacefully; and within the space of a few seconds, he grew aware of about eight things. He was lying on his back, and now he could see all of the old-fashioned Neapolitan bedroom, with its high ceiling and ornate wall decoration. He grew aware that he was in the bed under some very thin blankets with no clothes on, and lying next to him was a young, blond-haired, Diamondian woman.

He could see her bare shoulders protruding from under the blankets, and so he instantly surmised that she was naked also.

As he looked at her, she was lying in such a way that she was partially facing the other direction. But she must have heard his movement; for she turned and looked at him.

It was as he had, of course, analyzed, Isolina Ferraris.

For just a moment the tableau held. The two of them close together in the bed, not yet touching but gazing into each other's eyes. And then—

The young woman said, "Your remarks about a woman wanting love have stirred feelings in me which I thought I had buried for the duration."

Morton continued to gaze at her. He had been in bed with women before. When he was barely out of his teens he had accidentally discovered how to beat the women's unions . . .

The girl to whom he was engaged wouldn't leave her family's home planet when he was transferred. Being an experimenter, he had tested out the instant insight that brought him. Each time he had found himself an attractive home-attached girl, courted her, signed up to be her fiancé (which was actually a companionate marriage arrangement and not binding for two years). At the beginning of each relationship, the girl took it for granted that she would go along when he departed, but by the twentieth month the initial excitement was gone. She wouldn't leave her family. *She* broke the engagement. Since there was never any suggestion of ill-treatment or of any of the male chauvinisms that had brought the women's unions into existence, he was in the clear. No black mark against him. Free to find another fiancée on his new assignment.

Altogether, he played the game with nine fiancées.

Two things stopped the clever little scheme.

He began not to like what he was doing. That pure reaction was first, about four years ago. He had been sort of peacefully celibate for half a year when the second thing began to happen.

Women started accosting him on the street.

They actually connived to break through the union rules in order to have an affair with him.

Of course, he analyzed finally, *my body has gradually changed because I've been reasoning by finite logic almost every waking minute for two decades.*

It was one of several related phenomena known to a small but growing body of men and to a somewhat larger number of women.

The women who reached out to him in such a total fashion were finite logic females. And they were attracted to him because they recognized that he was becoming a finite logic male.

Unfortunately there were no such women on Diamondia.

But here was Isolina . . . He assumed from her intimate comment that velocity of lovemaking was not required of him.

She clearly wanted to establish a better image of herself in his mind.

While he permitted her to do so, maybe *he* could learn a few things.

Isolina was continuing, a faraway expression in her eyes, "When this war is over, I shall take the road to Damascus—do you know the allusion?"

Morton had to smile at her simplicity. It would never happen, of course. But he translated, "Back to morality and, I presume, to a lifetime of concealment of what is happening now. I suggest you move to Rome and get the bishop's blessing."

She laughed. It began as a tinkling, humorous sound, became slightly hysterical and ended on a bitter note. "I'm afraid my history is too widely known for concealment," she said.

The look on her face had changed again. When she spoke next, she seemed to have recovered her original calm—except her color was higher than Morton recalled it. She said in a practical tone, "Colonel, let me call us back to our duty. I shall feel more secure when I free you, knowing that you are out there with a memory of having possessed me. So—that's your situation. You can leave when you have done this thing."

So swiftly they were back to a kind of realism.

It was not exactly the mood and moment Morton had waited for. But it was an approximation. He said, "What did you find out from your father about the Gyuma Ravine?"

Surprisingly, she did not hesitate. "I called his headquarters," she said simply. "They say he's gone to the ravine. I didn't embarrass him by asking any questions of subordinates."

It sounded like an evasion, and yet her expression was unhappy. Hard to believe that her father would not have left open a line that could reach him anywhere. And yet there was a convincing sadness in her eyes.

Nevertheless, he couldn't leave such an important matter to mere surmise. He said, "If the disaster happened, what do you think of my friendly Irsk's belief that something Diamondian went wrong?"

The question did instant, twisting things to that beautiful face and body. All the muscles that he could see . . . rippled. "Diamondian males—" she began. She stopped as if the words threatened to strangle her. Then: "You can't imagine," she continued, "what those men are like. They are—"

Once more she couldn't go on. Again there was an automatic working of muscles deep in her body. "Oh, you can't imagine—" she repeated.

It was so visibly a kind of lifetime anguish and despair that Morton brought up his right hand, placed it on her bare shoulder and tugged. "You'd better come over here," he suggested gently.

The woman did not hesitate. She actually lunged at him. The skin to skin contact of their bodies literally started as a

51

blow. The next moment her arms were around him, pulling at him. "I don't know what you've done," she whispered, "but you've made this seem personal. Maybe for a change I can get something out of it, too, instead of being a pretending prostitute."

If her words were the scheme of a designing woman, it was skillfully done, indeed. Morton warmed at once, even in spite of having a cynical thought about it. As a result the act proceeded more naturally than he would have anticipated and came to its climax with him in a genuine state of excitement and the woman in an apparent one. He found himself actually reluctant to believe that her response was merely, as she had put it, the professional performance of a "pretending prostitute."

Isolina separated herself from him with a sigh. "Now *that*," she said, "*I* shall remember."

If it was pretense, it was damned good.

"Well—" Morton began. And stopped.

From somewhere in the house below them, a man screamed hideously. The sound was cut off at once. In the momentary dead silence that followed, Morton was aware that the woman's nude body had become rigid.

She was fast then. She flung the blankets aside and made a run for the dresser. And she actually was tugging at one of the drawers when the hall door burst open. All of the half-dozen Irsk, who glided through the opening in their equivalent of running, were armed with stubby little hand energy guns.

They could have burned her down. But one—obviously the leader—shouted, "Catch her! Hold her!"

What was astounding, then, was the speed of that getting. One moment, they were barely inside the door. The next two of the Irsk were beside the woman. And they had her, as they had been instructed. And held her.

Morton, who managed during those high speed movements to struggle into a sitting position, remembered Lositeen's instantaneous going up the stairway of his house.

Is it possible these people can do that anywhere?

The Irsk leader had been glancing around. Now he walked over to a chair, looked over at Morton and said, "Here are your clothes, colonel. Get dressed, and quick!"

There was no arguing with that tone. Approximately three minutes, Morton estimated, from getting out of bed to being fully clothed and shod. Not exactly a record for him, but close.

52

"Colonel, you're coming with us," said the Irsk. He turned to the others. "Okay all you dyl, let's go."

"What about the woman?" said one of them. "We killed everybody else. You're not going to leave her."

"Can't you see she's the girl friend?" was the irritated reply. "Use your head."

The other Irsk seemed to agree, but he said, "Don't you think we should see what she was after in that drawer?"

The drawer, opened, revealed two small automatic pistols. The two Irsk each took one. As they turned away, Isolina, who had been standing tensely, looked up and said, "Colonel Morton has had an experience with something he calls the darkness, which apparently transferred his perception into the mind of an Irsk."

Everybody had stopped. The Irsk leader said, "This is why we are taking Morton. He got more than anyone bargained for when that happened, and as a result we have a difficult problem to solve."

"In all the years," continued Isolina, "that the Irsk seemed to be friendly to the Diamondian people, there has never been the faintest inkling of such a phenomenon. What is this *darkness?* Why has it been kept a secret? And why did it place Colonel Morton's perceptions in the brain of an Irsk who is friendly to the Diamondians?"

"When we find that out," said the alien commander "we may have something to say to it, also."

The young woman persisted. "Then this is something that can be spoken of?"

They were all staring at her. Finally the leader gestured at Morton with one tentacle. To Isolina he said, "We're not giving you any information. The darkness is not for human beings."

By the time those words were spoken, Morton was walking out of the door. He was preceded by two of his captors. The remaining four followed him. The last one closed the door.

Ten

MORTON FOUND himself in a hallway that was also a stairwell with a skylight. The whole place, with its high, central dome effect, was brightly lighted by a brilliant chandelier that hung over the down stairs.

As he arrived at the head of the stairway, Morton stopped. Everything had been so rapid—even the getting dressed had provided no time for thought. Throughout, as he realized now, he had been intent on leaving the bedroom before these beings changed their minds and murdered the woman anyway.

But now—

He paused there and wondered: *What about me?*

In all these many hours he had been a puppet. The purposes of the blackness had possessed him. His brief apparent freedom in the hospital bed never had been convincing to him. Almost at once, the Diamondian conspirators had got him and totally controlled him until long after dark—What time was it? He guessed about eleven at night, or even midnight.

There had, of course, come those moments in bed with Isolina, when—presumably—he had some kind of choice. But here he was again, a full prisoner, this time of the Irsk rebels.

Is there anything I can do? Can I make any decision of my own?

Could he, perhaps, even discover why these Irsk needed to make him prisoner?

Without pausing, he asked the question. "What do you want with me, really?"

The reply of the Irsk leader was to point his "arm" tentacle downward. "That way!" he said.

Morton did not argue but headed, as directed, to the lower floor. And here he saw his first body. It was that of a middle-aged woman, whose style of dress suggested that she was probably a housekeeper or a maid. She lay crumpled at the foot of the stairs, and it was not obvious how she had been killed.

Arrived at the bottom of the steps, Morton obeyed another gesture by the leader and continued to walk toward—he guessed—the front of the house. A glance to his left through a wide alcove showed the sprawled bodies of half a dozen men and three women. That room was dimly lighted and in it were nearly a dozen Irsk. Morton's group came to a halt. The two Irsk units joined, and somebody in Morton's sextet said, "Where are the others?" "Still downstairs," was the answer. "We really trapped a nest of them down there. Altogether thirty-two men and eleven women in this house." The leader of the second group spoke with satisfaction.

"Good," said the leader of Morton's group. "But you'd better tell your dyl to come up. We've got who we came after." He indicated Morton.

"Hmmm!" The second Irsk paused, then: "I've called them." He now walked over in the gliding way of his kind and stood directly in front of Morton. He seemed about to speak, but it was Morton who uttered the first words. "I am a member of the Negotiating Committee. What do you want with me that we cannot discuss in a more cooperative environment?"

If the Irsk was surprised by the words, his smooth face did not show it. He addressed Morton in a formal tone. "Colonel, we have captured you for a non-negotiating reason. We know that a particular Irsk and you became mind-brothers. But we don't quite know how to undo something else that happened. That's why we need you along—so we can examine the problem and then do whatever is necessary."

Morton said, "What you did just now, when you silently called those others—I have the impression that you people communicate with each other by mental telepathy."

"It's not quite like that," said the Irsk. He tapped his head. "It takes the mind, yes; but what else is needed is a secret we have kept from human beings for a reason which even the green-striped Irsk friends of the Diamondian people accept without question."

"What's the reason?" asked Morton.

And waited tensely while the other hesitated. His feeling: his insight was about to meet a basic test.

The Irsk said abruptly, "The Diamondians are emotionally and mentally too unstable. They would wreck the system and so cannot be included in it."

Morton said in a taut voice, "These days, I understand, the rebel Irsk also seem to be wildly emotional."

His informant agreed grimly, "Our association with the Diamondian people," he answered, "has been inflammatory. A race which lived a totally peaceful existence is now as passionately violent as the Diamondians."

Morton said, "If what you say about the Irsk also being excitable is true, then why hasn't *that* wrecked your system of intermental communication?"

"Don't think it isn't shaking," was the retort. "That's one reason why we need you." When Morton expressed amazement, a tentacle waved him silent. "We'll talk about that later. Right now you're wanted on the ViewComm."

It was such an unexpected nonsequitur that Morton was momentarily speechless. Then: "*I* am wanted on the ViewComm?" he said, astounded.

But being in Intelligence, he said it to himself only. Silently, suspending bafflement, he walked into the indicated room. And then for long moments he stood, silent, gazing at the individual who looked out at him from the ViewComm.

The man on the screen had dark brown hair, gray eyes and a thin face with a sarcastic smile. Morton recognized him as Captain James Marriott of the Capodochino Corapo military post.

"Remember me?" asked Marriott's voice.

"Perfectly," said Morton in a hard voice.

But he grew thoughtful after he had spoken, because it was wrong for Marriott to *expect* to be remembered by Colonel Morton, who had only talked to him once, briefly.

Morton said that he would have expected to see Marriott on the Diamondian side and not the Irsk.

"I'm on all sides in this matter," was the reply, "perhaps even on yours, colonel. If life were forever," Marriott continued, "then no one would have to make a decision about where he would spend his remaining years. It was when I saw this Diamondian situation that it finally came to me that here I had found my place."

Morton had been hastily recalling the kind of interviewing he had done on his rapid exploratory tour of Diamondia those first days. He said, puzzled, "When I questioned you, what did I say that bothered you?"

"It wasn't any one question," Marriott replied. "It was your determination. I suddenly had the feeling that you meant business."

"Why didn't you mind-brother with me and find out what I was up to?" Morton asked.

There was a pause. Then: "For a reason," said Marriott, "I never became involved in that phenomenon. That's all I'll tell you. Anyway, I took the chance of tuning you into the Irsk energy network that you call the darkness in the hope that at a key moment I could control you." He grimaced. "That was the biggest mistake I ever made in my life."

"Was it you who had me sent to the hospital?" Morton asked.

"Yes."

"And when Isolina got me out for her own reasons—" Morton left the sentence unfinished.

"I was presently advised," was the reply, "and I sent the Irsk after you."

"Knowing that they would murder just about everybody here?" Morton flashed angrily.

The man in the viewplate shrugged. "I don't know what to say to that. Getting you was the important thing. I didn't tell them to do any killing. All these Irsk and Diamondians are loaded with murderous emotions. It's true that I opened the Irsk to differentiation ten years ago; so I guess I'm responsible to that degree."

He frowned. "They were all like one person to that thing up there in the sky. It actually had a billion Irsk lined up like duplicates. The first change I made was to set up an identification system based on emphasizing the pronunciation of everybody's name in a broad, exaggerated fashion. Unfortunately, as individuality expanded, the Irsk only had the Diamondians as examples. So my good deed was not well thought out."

"Anyway," he shrugged, "I said, 'Don't harm Isolina!' That's the best I could do. You see." He was suddenly grim. "Not one but two unfortunate things happened after I tuned you into darkness. The first was when it, without consulting anyone, mind-brothered you with Lositeen, the Irsk who controls the method which can destroy the darkness."

"What was the second?" asked Morton.

"That occurred when your subordinate visited me."

He explained unhappily about opening the door of Bray's car, confessed, "I was unaware. I got caught by a little gimmick. As a result an identity confusion was temporarily set up between you and me; and that, my dear colonel, is no joke. As a result of that something has to be done about you. Getting you off the planet might be enough, but I doubt it."

The somewhat pink face was earnest and tense. Morton had the uneasy feeling that Marriott believed what he was saying. He said, "Look, captain, if you're trying for peace here, I'm on your side. I want negotiations to resume—and, if you've made headway where we haven't, hell, man, I'll get

57

behind you and push. For God's sake, don't be secretive. Tell me what's wrong, and I'll cooperate to solve the wrongness."

Abruptly, the face on the ViewComm was sarcastic again. "What's happened here," said Marriott, "stirs men to other darker emotions than cooperation. What happened is that you replaced me as head of the Irsk government. Of the darkness, in short. What do you think of *that*?"

Ask a silly question, thought Morton, and you get the most fantastic answer ever offered in one continuous combination of words.

He grew aware that Marriott was speaking again. "Even though you haven't the faintest idea of how to take advantage of your preeminence," the man said, "I'm going to deduce that you will not lightly hand it over." He broke off angrily, "So what did you learn from Lositeen? Will you deign to share that with us?"

The man who stared up from the viewplate was visibly in a highly disturbed state. Morton himself was still off balance. He groped mentally for something to orient to. "Look," he said finally, reassuringly, "government is my specialty. I even have a degree in overthrow conspiracies. I admit," he went on more cautiously, "it's a little hard to picture the darkness as a government. But I can dimly imagine how it might be. If my picture is correct, then I foresee that the basic overthrow theory applies. If so, then I also know what the Lositeen Weapon, by theory, must be. It can only be—"

He stopped. Because Marriott was loudly saying, "Sssshhh!" and violently gesturing silence. The man's face on the screen was pale in a blotched way. "Colonel," he urged hoarsely, "don't say another word. The darkness can follow surface thoughts, particularly those that accompany a verbal statement. Don't give it any information."

Morton shook his head grimly, said, "Where an overthrow system can be used at all preknowledge of it is of no value to the government being overthrown. However, I'll keep my counsel on the details, if it'll make you feel any better. But remember, in science everything is automatic."

It must have seemed like the end of the conversation, for the Irsk subleader said to Marriott, "Captain, it's time Colonel Morton and I got on our way. This whole matter will be settled at top level. Goodbye, sir."

Marriott managed a twisted smile and said to Morton, "The darkness handled you as if it is no longer obeying its ancient Mahala programming. That implies a basic self-protect system about which I know nothing, but the principle of which is, when in doubt, destroy. Goodbye."

"Wait," said Morton. "You've used a new word. Mahala. What?"

He stopped. The viewplate had gone blank.

"This way," commanded his Irsk captor. "They're finally coming."

He motioned Morton out of the room.

The "they" was the third group from the basement, consisting of more than a score of individuals. They came from below, and as they clustered in large numbers in the hallway, it was evident that the members of the Irsk raiding party were about to make their getaway. And they were nervous about going outside.

So many of them, was the problem.

If they were seen in such numbers by the neighbors, or worse, if they had been seen entering, then . . . danger.

Morton stood by as, in a low-voiced conversation, the Irsk leaders of the three groups considered these matters. Swiftly, the trio decided to call all their cars at once. The vehicles had been sent over to park beside the botanical gardens, where— it had been reasoned—Irsk drivers would be as inconspicuous as anyone.

As Morton watched, fascinated, the cars were called by the same mental method. Apparently, then, as the vehicles approached the drivers signaled in a similar way; for suddenly the door was jerked open. Two Irsk grabbed Morton, and said to him, "Run for the second car!" He did not resist. He ran with them across a wide veranda, then over a broad, tree-lined lawn. It was, he noted unhappily, not only tree lined but shrub lined as well; so that the grounds were concealed from the neighbors.

Morton and the two guards who held him emerged from the gate onto the street, just as the first car with an Irsk driver pulled up in front of the house; the second car followed close behind. Within minutes he was being thrust into the rear seat of that second car. One of the guards scrambled in beside him, and the other climbed in beside the driver.

Other cars were pulling up behind the first two, and the rest of the Irsk were hurriedly getting into them. Morton was aware almost simultaneously of three things. Out of the corner of one eye, he saw that on the hillside was a large body of men. The men were Earth federation soldiers, and they had machine guns.

The third awareness was very simple. An Intelligence rule:

When you're in a confined space and see a lot of guns pointing your way, get down. Morton, without a word, almost as if he were a smooth, tentacled creature, slid to the floor of the car.

He lay there shuddering as the machine guns roared murderously. All around him was the sound of car motors revving up, as if some of the drivers actually were getting under way.

The machine he was in was not one of them. The Irsk in the car with him, as they realized the ambush, made an attempt to scramble to the ground. Morton presumed that each individual would utilize the Irsk high speed method of getting from one location to another. Who made it and who did not was not immediately clear.

Morton was still discreetly sprawled on the floor of the rear seat, when he became aware that someone had come up beside the car and was peering in.

Cautiously, he twisted his head and peered back—into the face of Lieutenant Bray.

The relief that came to Morton in that moment took a special form, which he expressed gratefully to his subordinate: "The deadly part of all this has been the helpless feeling of being under someone else's control. Now, at last—"

"But—" gulped Bray. He stopped; held back the horrid information that his only method of rescue had required that an arrest order be issued.

Later, Bray thought unhappily, I'll tell him . . .

Eleven

To BRAY, that morning, waiting at the rear entrance of the main hospital building, there had come a reluctant realization that something had gone wrong.

Struthers and he sat in the car, gloomily discussing possibilities, arriving finally at the conclusion that they would have to have assistance.

The question was, who would help a member of the Negotiating Committee?

He decided against asking for the help of the Committee itself. If it ever got out that the head of the Intelligence branch of the Negotiating Committee was in the process of getting himself involuntarily ejected from Diamondia—well!

He couldn't do that to Morton.

For the same reason, it seemed inadvisable to directly contact Earth federation headquarters. The innumerable Diamondian lovers over there had no use for the Negotiating Committee.

For a time, Bray pondered the problem gloomily. No plan occurred. Reluctantly, he had Struthers drive him back to the Negotiating Committee palace. There, with part of his mind still probing anxiously at Morton's dilemma, he went about doing in his fashion those duties which—he judged—would be valuable if and when.

There were five captains and three majors in the Intelligence section. Of these, one of the majors and two captains mildly enjoyed Lieutenant Lester Bray. Of the remaining two majors, one—his name was Sutter—disliked all lieutenants, but he had a special niche of hate in his heart for Bray, whom he considered brash and presumptious.

So it was with a certain amount of pleasure that Bray, later in the morning, approached this latter officer, and in his blandest voice reported that he had received a phone call from Colonel Morton during the night. ("The colonel didn't wish to disturb the sleep of upper echelon people like yourself, major.")

What Morton wanted, as Bray suavely outlined it, was information about the Diamondian peace delegation. Was anyone assigned to the task of searching cars in the Capodochino area?

Major Sutter had frosty blue eyes. He was the only officer who, when the Negotiating Committee arrived, had taken the trouble to move out the local office furniture and have brought in metal files, a metal desk and a metal chair. That these gleaming but plain items were out of place in that cunningly shaped room, with its delightful walls and a sense of space, did not seem to occur to him.

He had a clipped tenor voice that could have doubled for certain computer speaker systems. In this totally neutral and totally unfriendly voice, he said, "And when this information becomes available, *what* did Colonel Morton say should be done with it?"

Bray said, "He expects to be in his office late in the day, sir, and he would like to have the report on his desk by that time."

The lean body with the lean, tense face started to turn dismissingly away. "Very well, lieutenant, you may consider your message has been transmitted."

Bray held his ground. "What can I tell Sergeant Struthers to say to the colonel in the event that he phones and asks about the matter, major, sir."

Sutter was not about to be trapped by such a device. "As soon as I have some information," he replied in a formal tone, "I shall talk directly to Struthers and give him the requisite instructions. That is all, lieutenant."

"Thank you, major."

Bray saluted in the extra sharp, extra spit and polish, clickety-click style which he reserved for officers of this ilk. Whereupon he backed respectfully all the way to the door and out. And Sutter, who understood every nuance of what he was doing, hated him the more for it but still did not suspect that he had been given a message which had originated exclusively in the brain of Lester Bray, himself. Presumption on *that* level was outside Major Sutter's reality.

Bray now repeated the approach he had made to Sutter on Major Luftelet. There was nothing particularly dislikeable about Luftelet. He was a dull fellow. How, lacking sharpness, he had got into Intelligence was not obvious. Certain technical qualifications seemed to be his forte; he was a stickler on detailed information and usually made himself a little obnoxious in that department.

Again Bray took the attitude that it was Morton who wanted to know—this time about the exact nature of the building where Marriott had his otherwise minor, unimportant, village level military command post.

The older man sat behind one of the native desks, with its exquisite design like a waterfall in wood; and for several seconds he seemed to be staring off into the distances of his own soul. He radiated a kind of extra-sensitiveness, as if somehow inside him was a better person; a man who knew more, thought more clearly and felt things more keenly than lesser mortals.

It seemed sad to Bray when, after all that preliminary, there emerged from the pensive lips Luftelet's stereotype:

"What are your qualifications, lieutenant, for even discussing such technical matters."

"Sir," said Bray, "it is not my qualifications which are at issue. Naturally, I had to have certain trainings and a science degree—like everyone else here. But Colonel Morton will be the person who reads your report."

For a long moment, the other man's face was a study in

conflicting emotions. His expression silently questioned any-one's ability to comprehend what he knew. And yet he had the resigned look of someone who has come to realize that the world is a hard place for truth. His whole body now put forth an attitude of understanding that there were such people as superior officers, who held authorized positions which they might not be qualified for, but still—there they were.

In that resigned fashion, Luftelet said, "Very well, I shall make a, uh, summary of what this building can do. Mind you," he went on hastily in a severe tone, "this will not be a technical report, such as I might make to a person with my own training, but—"

He let the sentence hang; and Bray said, "I'm sure, major, you will not underrate Colonel Morton's numerous technical qualifications for understanding intricate electronic designs."

The darkness of that thought seemed to depress Luftelet. He nodded gloomily, and Bray took advantage of the result-ing silence to salute and depart.

Now what?

Wait, of course.

He sat at his desk in a small room, which he had early de-cided had once been a broom closet, and wondered if he had actually accomplished anything.

Thinking thus, he watched the minute hand move from twenty-three minutes after noon to ten minutes after six.

It was as twilight began to gray the world of Diamondia that Bray had had a simple thought: This thing needs a devi-ous solution. . . . He was momentarily stunned at not having realized it earlier. Because, of course, that was his way.

When he explained his plan to Struthers, that lantern-jawed individual looked startled and said, "Lieutenant, for God's sake, you'll have the colonel off this planet in record time if you don't watch out."

Bray was calm. "We need help. The way to get it is to set in motion the forces of law and order."

He had Struthers drive them back to the hospital. He was shortly engaged in a conversation with a certain Diamondian M.D. named Dr. Fondier, who became very excited when he discovered that a patient had taken it upon himself to depart from the hospital without being officially discharged.

It was he who indignantly set in motion the forces which brought Bray and the Earth federation soldiers to the house which the lieutenant eventually decided needed to be investi-gated.

Twelve

MORTON CRAWLED OUT of the back seat of the car and stood up. All around them were Irsk bodies. Morton shuddered and said, "Let's go inside."

Soldiers and technical people had already preceded them. As they entered, dead bodies were being carried up from the basement. Among the corpses Morton recognized George and Pietro, the only persons (besides Isolina) that he had actually seen in or connected with this house. There was no sign of Isolina. So he now sent Bray and a soldier upstairs to look for her.

She wasn't there. Shock! Anxiously he himself went up with Bray. He examined the bedroom in the hope that she might have escaped by some secret passage-way. That possibility yielded to a more practical thought when he discovered the direct route down to the back yard from the second floor—to a much greater concern.

Morton stood at the door and peered into the almost darkness of the alleyway. He thought: Suppose she went that way and ran into some of those escaping Irsk.

But an Earth federation unit sent to explore the narrow back street failed to find her body—or anyone else's. Which was relieving.

He was able at this point to review his own feelings. I deduce, he agreed grudgingly within himself, that she achieved her purpose by offering me sex. I am now personally interested in her welfare.

What interested him, he realized, was not so much the remembered warmth of her body but a kind of basic honesty and intelligence. Those direct questions she had asked of the killers indicated swift recovery from fear. It was pretty ridiculous, but he guessed by her own figures that she had had six or seven hundred different men in five years; and yet, he couldn't escape the—it had to be—irrational feeling that underneath it all she was a good woman.

Having had these thoughts, he was abruptly motivated to speak. "Wherever she is," he said, "if she had control of where it would be, she will be doing something rational. The young lady thinks on her feet, and acts according to where her reason takes her." He spoke with a hopeful note in his voice: "So if we could reason what insight a supremely intelligent, Diamondian woman would have had as a result of what she learned today, then we'd know where she headed when she left here."

He was aware of Bray giving him a sharp look. "You seem to have been impressed by that young lady, sir," said the younger man.

"I gather from your account of your visit to the Ferraris farm, that you were too," countered Morton.

It was true. "For a Diamondian," Bray began, "Isolina is—" Morton interrupted in a baffled tone, "Where would a sharply rational analysis take you on the basis of what I've told you?"

Bray had to admit reluctantly that he was not that rational.

The brief dialogue, having led to nowhere, ended.

Next: "That Lositeen situation—" Bray said. "After what you've just told me, we'd better find Lositeen and question him."

"A good idea," Morton agreed.

"Maybe I should get out there tomorrow," said Bray. "What's the name of that village?"

"I haven't the faintest idea," Morton replied.

Which ended that particular dialogue with finality. Morton turned with a decisive gesture, and said to Bray, "I suppose we can safely leave the cleanup here to the Earth federation forces."

The young officer paused to squeeze his eyelids before answering. And then waited while Morton squeezed his, also. Thereupon Bray winked at his superior and grinned.

It was such a carefree act, bespeaking continuing high energy, that Morton grinned back. Then, abruptly, his face hardened. "Let's go," he said. "There's a doctor in that hospital I want to check on, and maybe right now would be a good time, while I've got the military unit here to accompany me."

Bray held back. "Well, sir," he said diplomatically, "I guess this is the time to tell you one tiny fact that I've withheld."

His expression and tone were so odd that Morton, who had started to turn toward the door, slowly faced about and stared at him. "What is it?" he asked.

Bray told him, finished, "So you see, actually you're under arrest, presumably because that doctor is undoubtedly covering up for everybody."

They were standing near the top of the stairway as those

65

words were spoken. All around were the sounds and sights—and a rather gruesome smell—of cleanup: men in Earth federation gray green uniforms, bodies on stretchers, soldiers with mops and pails of water washing blood off the floors.

Morton watched the scene pensively, then turned to Bray and said with a forced smile, "Under the circumstances, lieutenant, what's to prevent you and me just walking off these grounds?"

"The whole area is surrounded," said Bray. "We'd be intercepted."

"Oh."

Bray continued in a judicial tone, "It will be interesting to see how all this comes out."

It was—Morton had to admit it, sort of savagely—a minimal comment on his own developing involvement on Diamondia.

Thirteen

STILL, HE APPRECIATED the reasoning that Bray had pursued. And so he was not depressed as, a little later, a motor platoon of federation soldiers escorted the car that carried Bray and himself. "I'll just have to confront these hospital authorities with Doctor Gerhardt," he said.

All around them was New Naples at night. Because of the war it was as dark as the devil's own hell—except for the incredible traffic. Everybody who had been out in his noisy little car in the daytime now seemed to be out in his little noisy car at night.

Worse, each person drove with dimmed lights through the otherwise Stygian dark streets. Good angels were everywhere presumably protecting the innocent and punishing the guilty. Each few minutes there was an appalling crash somewhere in the darkness, as some enemy of God met his fate.

In the darkness ahead, there was an earsplitting impact and the sound of steel crunching steel. The vehicle they were in gave a lurch and came to a dead stop.

From somewhere near curses mingled with unhappy voices in a rising crescendo of blame and counterblame. Horns began to blow maddeningly.

"Well—" said Morton again, more purposeful now.

He peered through the glass of the car into the darkness. Ahead and to the right were dim shapes of cars standing still. In the lane immediately to his left cars were moving slowly, blowing their horns. Farther to the right buildings of the old style were visible like gloomy wraiths in a universe of dark shadows. In an hour or so, thought Morton, the big moon of Diamondia would poke up above the eastern horizon and bathe this spooky scene in its bright, revealing radiance. But at this moment, with this noise blaring—

As he had the awareness, the horns became positively hysterical. And so it was now or never.

Softly, Morton opened the car door and tugged gently at Bray's arm. For a tiny, startled moment that young man resisted. But instants after that they had both stepped down to the pavement on the right, clutching each other, felt their way through a tangle of stopped vehicles, and so to the comparative safety of the sidewalk where the gloomy buildings were. They began to walk rapidly.

"We'll phone the hospital in the morning," Morton said. And then he added, "Maybe." He was kind of mad and kind of fed up and not too willing to be reasonable with unreasonable people. But it wasn't over, he realized wearily.

It occurred to him, as he suddenly observed his mood, that he was in a state of modern logic irritation. "My professor," he said, "used to drill us in finite logic reactions. His attitude was that you could always tell people who still had the old modern logic attitudes by their emotional response when something went wrong. Such individuals, according to my professor, deep down inside believe that there is, in fact, such a thing as a set, a collection of duplicates. If they could ever get over that, he said, they would discover that science is infinitely variable but automatic. Every process is slightly different from all other processes, but what it is, it *is*."

He broke off. "What we have here on Diamondia is a single remaining puzzle. By theory, if we solve that puzzle the consequences will follow automatically, a kind of instant victory."

"I hate to say it," said Bray respectfully, "but instant victory on a whole planetful of Diamondians and their duplicates, the Irsk, sounds absolutely impossible."

"Well—" said Morton, "at first look that would certainly seem to be true. Five hundred million passionate Diamondians and a billion unstable Irsk . . . Still, there's a kind of purity about all those people."

Bray said that the term *pure* didn't describe any male Diamondians that he had ever met. "Maybe the women——" He added hastily, "But I wouldn't know about that. I've stayed away from Diamondian females."

This time, Morton ignored the interjection.

"What bothers me," he said fretfully into the night, "is that mind-brother concept. At no time was Lositeen aware that I was there inside his skull, watching the world through his eyes. Yet Marriott and his Irsk friends knew that the darkness had put me there. Both with you and with me, Marriott showed extreme disturbance: anger, frustration, sarcasm. Yet the Irsk talked to him civilly and acted as if the matter of my deposing him is not finally settled. I was to be taken somewhere and questioned, and presumably at that time a decision would be rendered. I'm going to deduce from those facts that one of these hours, I also am going to have to make a choice. And so," he mused, "the main question is . . ."

Bray walked along, waiting for the completion of Morton's thought. After many seconds of polite silence, the younger man raised his voice to compete against the traffic roar, saying, "I'm anxious to hear, sir, what the real question may be."

No answer.

Bray stopped short in the darkness of that strange duplicate city. Tentatively, already silently cursing himself, he extended his arm and hand into the near night. Swung it gently in a wide sweep. There was no one; only the warm, tropical air caressed the skin of his hand and rippled his uniform.

Bray stood very still, striving to remember: *Did I hear anything, did I see anything, after he spoke?* . . . Darkness has many shades. The shade on Diamondia at this moment was a total black, alleviated only by car-light reflections. And those reflections were astonishingly useless in a city that had so many dull surfaces.

Yet as Bray remembered it he had been occasionally aware of the shape of the older man vaguely silhouetted—against what was not obvious. Dark against dark? It seemed impossible.

He was carefully retracing his footsteps as he had these rapid, desperate, private thoughts. With each step, he swung his foot over a good six-foot arc close to the invisible surface of the sidewalk.

It was amazing, then, to discover how far he had walked. His roving foot did not touch an inert body until he had gone at least fifty yards.

Who was it? Morton, he was fairly certain. He knelt beside the body and ran his fingers over the smooth cloth seeking familiar buttons, epaulets, the insignia of a colonel. They were all there. So it had to be Morton.

His fingers sought and located a limp wrist. Felt and found the pulse—it was slow but steady. Bray estimated, a strong sixty; and thereby felt great relief and the beginning of compassion.

This poor guy, he thought . . . Morton had now been in a state of enforced unconsciousness almost continuously for a day and a half. It seemed like too much for one human being. To the anxious young aide, the conviction came that such a total of bad luck and quantity of unconsciousness meant that Morton would not long survive.

And still he was only deducing that the body lying so unmoving here in this darkness was, in fact, Colonel Charles Morton. I swear, Bray whispered mentally to himself, that in future I shall carry on my own person all those small items recommended for Intelligence officers, like the tiny, brilliant flashlight that he had in his car, and other remarkable scientific marvels.

Being young and cocky and sophisticated, he had disdained cluttering his pockets and the linings of his uniforms with such things. And so—

No radio, no weapon, no police call, no—name it, and he didn't have it. In his car, yes, but not on him.

He *could* make a phone call from a public phone—if he could find a public phone in this darkness.

He didn't even try to look for a booth. Simply, he sat down beside the still but breathing body. Bray gloomily took it for granted that he would have to wait until dawn. Lacking Morton's special attention to certain details, he didn't know that the great Diamondian moon or at least a quarter of it, would shortly peak over the old style, Neapolitan roofs. And so he had that sudden pleasure after a mere thirty minutes. First the warning glow; the happy realization. And then the yellow crescent, like a dim fraction of a second sun, brightened the whole world around him as it sent its slanting rays along the avenue.

The light, somewhat ironically, revealed that there was a phone booth only twenty feet away.

A minute then to drag Morton's body into a darkened doorway. And then—

Bray phoned the palace in which the Negotiating Committee had its headquarters. The phone computer switchboard connected him with Sergeant Struthers' room; and that sleepy baritone voice eventually came on the line . . .

Struthers, driving a Committee station wagon arrived over an hour later. Which obviously was fast transportation in that traffic. With a few grunts and much heavy breathing, the two men carried Morton to the car and so brought him to the palace and Bray's bedroom. They undressed the limp body, laid it on the bed and put a sheet over it. Then Lieutenant Bray, who had been thinking in his fashion, explained to Struthers something of his plans for the next day and sent that worthy individual, pale but resigned, back to bed.

Fourteen

THE WAVE OF DARKNESS had come to Morton in another of its five minute intervals. It was bigger, but he was talking and intent; so he merely paused to squeeze his eyes.

Then blankness.

He seemed, if anything, to be suspended in a visionless void. Like a blind man, perhaps, yet not quite that. There was gray rather than black.

Morton was mentally still walking along beside Bray on a New Naples street at night. The transition from a black to a gray world wasn't all that different.

What confused him, then, was that he could . . . feel . . . what seemed to be his living body. Morton put his hand out, as if he would pull aside the curtain of grayness; and he opened his mouth and said uneasily, "Where am I? Lieutenant Bray, are you there?"

He was about to say more, when he realized a startling thing. There had been no sound . . . the feel of speaking. His mouth, jaws, tongue moving. Consciousness of a face above it and of a body below.

But not a whisper, not an echo.

Deathly silence.

Morton struggled against panic. Then had another awareness: a sense of distances around him; a faint sprinkle of stars to one side.

Oh, he thought then, I'm up *here* . . .

He ceased his writhing and held still. His belief was that he

70

was in process of being mind-brothered. He wondered: Will it be with Lositeen again?

He couldn't escape the weary feeling that all this was a waste of time. Problems among disagreeing groups were resolved by negotiation. And, damn it, why didn't these people get together and present their reasonable demands?

Time passed. Not too long. Another minute, perhaps. Suddenly, a baritone voice spoke directly inside his head, "Colonel Charles Morton, what seems to be alive up here is an energy duplicate of that body. It is this energy duplicate which can, in effect, speak and hear speech. The fact that your real body is unconscious is another reason why human beings cannot normally be admitted to the Irsk mental community. Irsk, when subjected to a message level energy impulse, do not lose consciousness. Thus, their duplicates can interact back and forth. And what they say and do is perceived by the real body on the planet below."

. . . Relief. Intense, almost mind-shaking relief. It seemed to Morton that he was being given genuine information. At last, he thought, a sensible being to talk to. He talked— quickly:

"I welcome your explanation," he said. "The human unconsciousness would appear to be a minor problem of impedance, which you should be able to resolve . . . Did you overhear my conversation with Captain James Marriott?"

"Yes. That's why you're here this time. I'd like you to analyze the Lositeen Weapon for me."

Morton said, "Oh!" And was silent. Just like that, he sensed inexorable purpose.

Nothing sensible here.

He hesitated and then decided once more on straight-forwardness. He explained, "Now that I visualize this vast energy field up here as a government, my knowledge of government overthrow theory tells me that you are not yourself the darkness not the government. You are only a segment of it."

He went on in the same reasonable tone. "I was told that a human being was head of the Irsk government. Now, I—another human—have replaced him. Obviously, by analogy, you must be a department control center. In a goverment as I know it, there would be many such departments. I deduce from your preeminent position that you must be connected with the communication lines of the government and are subject to programming which requires you to take over in an emergency. Is that correct?"

71

The answer came right into his brain as before. It was the same neutral voice. It said, "Colonel Charles Morton, I did not activate your duplicate in order for you to receive information from me. Before I release you, you will do two things for me. You will analyze the Lositeen Weapon. And you will promise to help me exterminate the Diamondian people. Do you agree?"

The words came into a mind that was already braced to maintain itself against a fantastic environment. But that sudden meaning was beyond *all* the previous reality of the Diamondian dilemma. Long pause. Stunned shock. Then an initial tiny reaction:

Automatic, thought Morton. *Not a sign of rationality.*

During the numerous hours that followed he refused without qualification to make any agreement about the Diamondians. But in a half-panicky need to maneuver for time while he considered some way of manipulating the total insanity of this being, Morton did what he had intended to anyway: analyzed the Lositeen Weapon.

"A government," he said, "is maintained by an agreeing citizenry and by a bureaucratic apparatus. Right now you, who are some aspect of that bureaucracy, continue to operate as if your government is still in existence. It's as if the elected government has been wiped out, but the tax collector still sends out his bills, and the courts continue to hear civil and criminal cases. Not everybody pays and not everybody shows up for trial, but there's a kind of feeling among the populace that all those government buildings and employees are still real.

"Where the government is an energy field," Morton continued, "I analyze that I, as nominal head, am attached to an energy center, which is the point of control; and I further analyze that I cannot be physiologically detached by a department head such as you are. But so long as I don't know how to manipulate that control center—and I don't—a segment of the control center, *you*, can act for the darkness . . . If you will affirm or correct what I have just said, I shall continue with my analysis of the Lositeen Weapon."

Pretty clever, thought Morton. Will he (it) fall for my apparent need for information in connection with my analysis which it (he) wants?

The baritone voice said, "Your analysis is exactly true."

It could have been under other circumstances a moment of triumph. Not under these. Not here, with his real body lying unconscious on the sidewalk at night in New Naples; and with his self somehow able to think inside an energy duplicate of that body.

Morton swallowed his anxiety and kept on. "A conqueror, who took over a country," he said, "in the old days used to set up direct military control of the conquered nation. It was not easy. Patriots were everywhere, fighting the occupation troops. Revolts were frequent, needing to be suppressed by force of arms.

"That method has been replaced by a method invented by the early communist theoreticians. This replacement system requires each citizen of the conquered country or planet to make a choice. The old government is not removed. Its leaders, unless there is some reason to try a few individuals for crimes, are usually treated with courtesy and are normally not harmed."

He continued, "The conqueror sets up an apparatus to which he gives some innocuous name like Political Education Center. The power of such a PEC derives from the simple, stark reality that presently it controls all the jobs in the country.

"Nobody has to go to PEC . . . that is, if they don't mind not eating or not having a place to live. Each citizen soon discovers where he must go for food and shelter. After watching his wife and family starve for a while and after experiencing a few hunger pangs himself, he hauls down the patriotic flag in his heart and humbly goes into town and registers with PEC.

"Obviously," Morton concluded, "the Lositeen Weapon will be an Irsk equivalent of a PEC, Political Education Center. You can see that knowing about such a system in advance is no protection against it."

"Has such a system been used recently to take over planets?"

"Only in remote areas of space, which have not after colonization established contact with the Earth federation. In such isolated instances, human beings go through their automatic behavior patterns, and soon somebody who feels that one or the other system is right bloodily enforces what he believes in—though never these days, when the methods are so well known, as bloodily as in the old times."

Morton continued, "When we find such situations, one of my jobs has been to topple the paranoid and to establish what is today almost everywhere accepted: the individual's right to choose periodically which system he wishes to live under—private enterprise or community enterprise. On Diamondia

73

such a choice system never got started. There's never been a movement among the Diamondian people in its favor, presumably because of the vast supply of cheap Irsk labor. That completes my analysis," he said.

"I analyze," said the voice, "that our first step must still be that you help me exterminate the Diamondian people. Then I will help you win the election against Marriott, and then—"

It was too much. Morton said in a strained voice, "For God's sake, how can one man help anybody to destroy five hundred million human beings?"

"—And then," concluded the baritone voice, as if it had not heard his interruption, "between the two of us we shall gain control of the Lositeen Weapon."

Once more Morton thought shakily: *It really is automatic.* He parted his duplicate lips to tell this utterly remorseless thing where it could go, when a meaning from it, that he had not noticed, penetrated.

"Election!" he yelled. "What election?"

"Everyone is puzzled at the method by which you became attached to the control center of the Irsk government. Captain James Marriott has explained it as an indentity confusion, artificially created. But this is a difficult concept for an Irsk, who has his own identity in his name. You are both to be questioned, and then the Irsk nation will render a majority decision. The Irsk have never been wholly satisfied with Captain James Marriott because he seems to have private purposes."

For a man trained as was Morton, there was a lot of information in the great being's words. But he discreetly held silent, trying even to avoid thinking about it.

The baritone voice continued, "I am confident that your election would be certain if you agree to help me exterminate the Diamondian people. Captain James Marriott refuses to do that—"

The feeling that surged inside Morton as that deadly purpose was presented for the third time was strictly modern logic—irrational. Foolish, he knew, for anyone to get mad at a machine. His voice shot up, nevertheless, and he yelled, "You can go straight to hell, you murderous bastard."

"I," said the darkness, "shall ask you periodically to change your mind. As soon as you do so, you will be allowed to return to your own body."

When those words had been spoken, a great silence descended upon Morton, where he seemed to be poised in empty space.

In all the time that followed the silence was broken only occasionally, as the baritone voice asked him, "Have you come to a decision?"

And each time Morton answered in a steady voice, "No change."

Fifteen

THE THING TO REMEMBER about a Diamondian woman, Isolina Ferraris had often told herself, is that she has been forced for centuries to associate with Diamondian males. Her observation: Such a man was too much for a woman. There were no exceptions, not even in her case.

Yet there were minutes, sometimes hours, when she was unwary. After the Irsk took Morton to the lower floor of her family's town house in New Naples, Isolina hastily dressed, found another pistol, slipped out into the hallway and tiptoed to the ramp that led down to the yard from the second floor. Moments later she was running along the alleyway to where her own car was always parked for a quick departure.

Soon she was relatively safe in the scrambling traffic of a wide thoroughfare. And the question became, where should she go? Whom should she contact first?

Her unwary impulse was to seek out her father. Being a general's daughter, her car had special equipment aboard. So it required only thought. After a mere hesitation or two, she spoke the fateful words that connected her with his headquarters. This time she had her call put through to his field office near the Gyuma Ravine. When the familiar voice came on the ViewComm—the picture was shut off, which meant he was probably in bed with a woman—she told him what had happened. What was unexpected by the daughter was that she was suddenly tearful about some of the people who had been murdered.

It was as if her father had been waiting all these years for his daughter to show a sign of weakness, or as he would have put it, of womanliness. In seconds, his voice peaked in the Diamondian male fashion. He screamed at her to the effect that she must now recognize that it was time for her to go to the family palace and abide there in the subdued, withdrawn fashion of a woman.

Isolina listened to the insanely screeching voice, and thought: Poor papa, he is really worried. But she was also startled. For he was not a man who merely spoke words. He acted. And what he was yelling as he finished was that he would send an airborne unit over to the farm, and she would be flown home "this very night." His final words were, "Stay at the farm until they come, and you obey your father, understand!"

It was a typical Diamondian male approach to the woman thing. And what was also typical was that he broke the connection before she could give him an argument.

After that, naturally, she could not go to the farm.

But she had an idea: Marriott . . . All these months, she thought, I have been puzzled about that man. Now she had a good excuse.

And so, in due course, she was giving her name to a guard at the door of the ugly Earth federation post in Capodochino Corapo. Less than a minute later Captain Marriott came hurrying along the corridor in his robe. His face was paler than she remembered, and in his eyes was a haunted expression. Nevertheless, he made a great show of concern for her. He had a corporal take her to the same spare room that Bray had occupied two nights before.

He himself ostentatiously got dressed and then had a guard knock on her door and bring her to his office, where he had a drink waiting for her. Isolina was amused by these token acts of courtesy. She analyzed that they were designed to protect her reputation but not her. For her, it was prostitute night, with Jimmy as the customer.

At least she would have a place to stay, and, at last, a legitimate reason for being inside the post, with her first real opportunity to spy on a man about whom she had become progressively curious. It was Marriott who had arranged the first peace meeting between the Diamondians and the Irsk at the Gyuma Ravine and was now arranging a second.

Sitting there in his office, watching his tense, too thin face, she told him almost everything. She omitted principally the sex act with Morton. She repeated exact sentences spoken by the Irsk and by Morton about the darkness.

She had been sipping her drink as she spoke. Now, her story completed, she leaned back in her chair, feeling suddenly quite sleepy . . .

Sixteen

BRAY HAD REMAINED in the room with Morton's body.

Whistling softly, he removed the colonel's insignia from Morton's uniform, and pocketed it. His superior's kit and billfold followed.

Then he lay down on the floor and, for a while, listened to the sounds of the Neapolitan night which came through the open window. The distant roar of autos was a steady throb in his brain. And nearby he heard the chirping of night birds, which, along with almost all other creatures of Earth, the Diamondians had brought to their new planet.

Somewhere in there, Bray slept like a good lieutenant should.

Next day—

Morton's body remained unchanged. It lay on the bed, breathing softly. No sign of consciousness. And not the faintest clue as to where he was this time.

In Lositeen's mind? Somehow Bray doubted it.

For the benefit of the Irsk maid, Bray pinned a note on his door: DO NOT CLEAN THIS ROOM UNTIL FURTHER NOTICE.

As he strode along the broad corridor, he began to meet other officials, and there was that usual polite exchange of amenities. The staff of the Negotiating Committee consisted of approximately seven hundred males. The clerks and lower level employees shared rooms with one or more others of their ilk. Officers and upper civilian personnel occupied the innumerable separate rooms of the grand palace, one to a room. Already, Diamondian prostitutes had penetrated here; and some of these aggressive young things were now boldly emerging from various rooms and heading for the nearest exits.

Bray avoided the purposeful looks which a few of the girls directed toward him. "Maybe arrangements for tonight?" one rather pretty creature suggested. Bray walked on, ignoring her. Where he would be by evening, in fact, where he would be by noon, was God's secret, as a Diamondian would say.

Besides, he was wary of getting involved. Every day at

77

least three members of the Negotiating Committee failed to show up for work.

No one knew what happened to them.

At first, for Bray, it was his usual morning. Eat quickly in the junior officers' commissary. Back then to his own office at the rear of the palace. Scan the news tapes with their battle reports from the Diamondian-Irsk front.

It seemed that, after a quiet which had pretty well lasted since the arrival of the Negotiating Committee, a severe battle was developing in a hitherto unaffected region called the Gyuma Ravine.

Bray was impressed. So that was what had resulted. Momentarily, a sadness came. Could it really be another of those damned Diamondian madnesses, as Lositeen had so instantly surmised, that had turned a peace talk into carnage?

The melancholy lasted only moments. He surfaced almost at once. An optimistic thought. Lositeen knowing of the carnage apparently within minutes of its beginning—that was the significant item. People would forever be people but when something that looked like mental telepathy was claimed not to be . . . what then?

Still thinking about it, Bray began to open his mail.

Nothing of interest.

He had set the arrival of the mail as the dividing line—between what and what, he wasn't sure. In a way he was waiting for something to happen that he could grab hold of and make happen harder.

He remembered an item of his conversation with Morton, and he prepared a memo:

> TO: All Personnel,
>   Negotiating Committee
>
> FROM: Colonel Charles Morton.
>
> We have received several reports, which indicate that a number of persons are suffering from an ailment that has the following symptom: The afflicted individual experiences periodic blackouts but is otherwise undisturbed. People so affected have a tendency to squeeze their eyes tightly shut—

Bray paused, pen poised. It struck him that if, when, Morton regained consciousness, the identification of eye squeezing as an illness might be embarrassing. So he stroked out that sentence, completing the memo thus:

78

Any person so afflicted should report immediately to Colonel Morton or Lieutenant Bray. Do not—repeat NOT—see a doctor at this time.

Presently, through Struthers, the corrected version was at the instant printing and distributing center; instant in this sense meaning that in about five minutes it would be on everybody's desk.

Well, almost everybody's. Bray thought it advisable to omit Mr. Laurent and his absolute top aides from the communication line.

Bray sat back and waited. Six minutes . . . ten . . . twenty. Nobody came in to report himself as a victim. The reality of that became startling. Was it possible, could it be that only Morton was being used by the darkness?

Under the circumstances, it was unfortunate that he had but one clue to the location of the little town where Lositeen had his job; what Morton had told him of his vague memory of having seen the place before.

After additionally culling over his conversation with Morton the previous night, Bray called in a rather high echelon bright young man named Kirk, who loved Diamondian prostitutes. Bray presented Kirk with the problem of locating an Irsk called Lositeen who worked in a hardware store in one of two hundred towns which—Bray concluded—"You will find listed in the itinerary file of Colonel Morton's recent tour."

His evaluation of the young clerk as being bright was, alas, immediately born out. The rather plump, sensuous face acquired a wise expression. The head, with its bulky brown hair, began to move back and forth in a negative headshake.

"Sir," said the soft voice, "about ten minutes after we start calling, both the Diamondians and the Irsk will be apprised of what we're doing. What kind of trouble do you think we might run into once they find out?"

Bray frankly didn't know. But it occurred to him that it would be unwise to let the Diamondians discover that a specific Irsk was being searched for.

"Let me think about it," said Bray.

Kirk turned to go; then hesitated and turned back. "I've often intended to speak to you," he said. "How about going on the town with me this evening. I've already got a prostitute arranged for myself for tonight. Why don't I phone her and get one of her roommates for you, and we'll make a double date."

79

Bray recalled vaguely hearing that Kirk came from an important family. So he didn't hesitate. Making dates was not a problem for him. It was keeping them that was often difficult. He said, "Okay."

When Kirk had gone, Bray phoned Dr. Gerhardt, the psychiatrist. He identified himself as Colonel Morton to the secretary who answered and was relieved to learn that Gerhardt was not in his office.

Thus, still representing himself to be Morton, he was able to apologize for his failure to show up and to say that he would call again and ask for another appointment.

Pleased, Bray hung up; and it was as he leaned back in his chair that he felt slightly dizzy. He closed his eyes, squeezed them hard and thought: Boy, I must really feel under pressure!

A few minutes later he had the same dizzy feeling. Again he squeezed his eyes. It was as he opened them that he *noticed what he had done.*

Fear!

Exactly how long he fought the silent, shaking battle to recover his stability, he had no clear idea. His eyes did the compulsive squeeze several times. Eventually, he was able to walk unsteadily into the adjoining bathroom. There he washed his face with cold water.

He returned to Morton's desk, sat down and braced himself. All right, so I've got it, also. Now what?

As he sat there, the minutes of the morning raced on; and there was no answer to that question either in his mind or from an exterior source.

But, feeling drained and in need of something—what was not clear—he did go out with Kirk at the end of the work day.

Seventeen

AFTER LEAVING the Negotiating Committee's palace, Bray and Kirk took an Irsk taxi, which, Kirk explained, would deposit them on a street in "modern" New Naples. There Kirk would meet his prostitute of the evening, a good-looking Diamondian named Marian. She would have another girl with her for Bray. *Her* name was Maria.

He warned Bray, "You will have a problem with Maria. She will be angry, like most Diamondian prostitutes." Marian (he continued) had been like that the first Thursday. That's who she was: his Thursday night girl. Naturally he didn't want her to learn that he had other girls in other parts of the city for the remaining six evenings. If she found out, she might become difficult again.

"That first Thursday night," he said, "she gave me what I paid for. Availability but no tenderness." He continued, "The second Thursday, my first night's energetic courtship and my innuendo about my wealth paid off. She was friendly. Tonight we should have a complete surrender."

Bray had become progressively uneasy as the other man developed his thesis. That's all I need, he thought. To the tension he was already under, add one hostile girl.

Like innumerable young men growing up in Man's galaxy, he had spent his most stimulated years confronting a closed shop, female union. The system had barred him from all but three jittery young females and half a dozen older women. Each of these nervously offered him a one-time association, in every instance a consequence of chance: for the necessary two hours, Big Sister was not watching. Under the tense circumstances, five of his nine performances, including all of the last three, had been partial disasters. The memory had faded with the passage of five months (since the last time). In accepting Kirk's invitation, he had taken it for granted that since there was no women's union on Diamondia, he would not be affected by any girl's attitude.

Suddenly he was not so sure. Suddenly he was appalled by the possible outcome. If he failed with Maria, she'd tell Marian, who would inform Kirk. Somehow it might spread to the staff of the Negotiating Committee. Certain people would be very happy to hear of his difficulties.

His brain raced anxiously over the possibilities and came up first with a temporizing question. "Why are Diamondian prostitutes angry?" he asked.

"It's a one up thing," said Kirk: "Just imagine, they get all the sex and all the men a girl could ever dream of having. And get paid for it. But they can blame the men for being the kind of beasts they are. It's a perfect setup for a girl—you'll agree?"

Bray was startled. Kirk's was an attitude he had never run into before. No time to consider it now. Now he had a thought of his own. He said, "Why don't we play a little game on Marian and tell her that I'm you and you're me?"

"What's that for?" The sensuous, slightly bulgy face looked puzzled.

"Will she then feel compelled to turn her friendship toward me?" urged a hopeful Bray.

Kirk said, "Hey, that's brilliant."

Bray waited, trying to appear modest. But he had to fight an inner battle against excessive self-admiration.

"I can see," grinned Kirk, "you're as cynical about women as I am—" He broke off, "Sounds like the greatest little game I've heard recently."

Bray, who had in his brief years of maturity reaped his share of the whirlwind of earlier generation male con games against women, had never had an opportunity to become cynical.

But a game player he was. He said, "I'll be Kirk, and you be Bray. We'll act as if so far you've been sort of my agent." He urged, "It might be interesting."

"It will make the evening," said Kirk, grinning.

He drew out his billfold and quickly handed over a large sum of money. "Remember," he said generously, "this whole evening is on me. But you appear to pay for everything and give me back later what's left over."

Moments after the transaction was concluded, Kirk pointed ahead, "There they are." Bray followed his finger and saw two girls standing near the curb. Both were rather suggestively dressed in short overalls, one in blue and one in red. The taxi pulled up, and the two men bounced youthfully out. Kirk introduced Bray.

Marian was the one in blue. She was an exceptionally good-looking girl of about nineteen and a half. Her friend Maria was a slightly plumper specimen, but she was also good looking and appeared to be only a few minutes older than her companion. As Kirk had predicted, the principal difference between the two girls was that Maria was hostile and unsmiling, whereas Marian lovingly kissed Kirk.

The two men had agreed that the switchover would be attempted about midevening. They paired off accordingly and headed to begin with to the Restaurant Corsica, where the cover charge was the equivalent of eight federation dollars per person, and the dinners started at twelve federation dollars. The entertainment was provided by well-known opera singers.

Until Kirk, Marian had cleverly never been taken to the Corsica. It was apparent to Bray that, being little more than a child, she was already having fantasies about this member of the Negotiating Committee finding her charms more than ordinarily attractive; and she might even be visualizing herself as the future Mrs. David Kirk.

It was evident that the somewhat plump con man Kirk, who had the money and the leisure to work for effects like that, thus received from normally antimale, Diamondian prostitutes a sincere affectionate response, with the warmth of real feeling and a total desire to please. All seven of his prostitutes—one for each night of the week—had already bought the same bill of goods. At least he had told Bray that they had. So, as Bray watched, Kirk was spontaneously kissed, erotically touched and inspired and in several ways prepared for a night of physical delight.

After the gourmet dinner, the two couples went to the San Carlo Theater, because Kirk—over and above his fleshly wants—was a connoisseur. And in his eyes the San Carlo was a reproduction of an old Neapolitan theater so breathtakingly beautiful that in a flash the garbage outside the door, casually dropped by a passing Diamondian, became of no importance. He whispered to Bray that Diamondians had undoubtedly been creating beauty next to garbage from time immemorial, while they lived their dark inner lives.

The San Carlo Theater was ornate, yes; and its shows were somewhat garishly aimed to provide Earth federation forces with a kind of pop opera. But still the music and the performance had the distinctive Diamondian touch; and that was good enough for Kirk and his prostitute of the night. Even Maria showed animation and several times deposited herself happily in Bray's lap.

It was during the intermission in the San Carlo that Kirk made the announcement: "Girls, my friend and I have a confession to make."

He thereupon told the story exactly as Bray had outlined it.

It took a while for the meaning to sink in. The two girls both frowned and twisted their faces, as they struggled with the concept. "You mean—" It was Maria who spoke first to Bray, "You are he?" She indicated Kirk.

Marian protested to Kirk, "But—I have known you for three weeks."

"Yes, but I'm not me," said Kirk. "I'm him." He pointed at Bray.

Suddenly it must have penetrated. The girl got a stunned look on her face. She had been sitting on the older man's lap.

Now she walked over and slumped into her own chair. She gave Bray a stricken look. "*You* are David Kirk?"

Bray nodded cheerfully. "I usually send Bray here," He indicated Kirk, "to look over a new city for me. He told me about what a wonderful girl you are. So I hope you don't mind switching over to me, because I'm the one that's paying his way, and I'll be paying for the evening, too, of course—okay?"

There was a silence—broken by Maria. "Of course, it's okay. We are girls of the street, Marian and I; and we sleep with who pays. That's right, isn't it, Marian?"

Marian was visibly bracing herself. She glanced at the real Kirk. "It is all right with you?"

"That's what I was out here for," he answered cheerfully, "looking for a girl that, uh, my boss, David here, would really go for."

The evening was visibly not quite as great for Marian after that. She tried. She laughed a lot. She stroked Bray's cheek and kissed him just as lingeringly as, earlier, she had kissed Kirk. But her eyes didn't look normal.

The slightly less than gay celebrants arrived a few minutes after eleven at the apartment building in which Marian and Maria shared rooms with another prostitute. Bray paid the driver of the taxi. It was as he turned to accompany his companions that he saw Kirk squeeze his eyes hard. He was instantly startled. There had been no previous sign in Kirk to indicate that he also had Morton's malady.

The truth was that the plump young man himself thought nothing of the phenomenon until five minutes later, after they had walked up to the fourth floor, the same blackness and the same eye-squeezing reflex brought a sudden recall of the memorandum of that morning from Colonel Morton on this very subject.

The shock was terrific, for the implication in Morton's memo had been that the affliction was a kind of disease. Kirk was not a man to let mere illness spoil his night. But it was disconcerting to have the darkness move like a pulse wave through his brain every five minutes while he was trying to perform the sex act upon a cooperative Diamondian girl.

Still, like Morton and Bray before him, he was adjusting to the inconvenience when suddenly a somewhat longer wave of blackness struck.

Maria had already in her brief career had an aged customer die on top of her of a stroke; and so the sudden dead

84

weight of the man brought a sharp fear. "Mr. Bray—" she whispered.

No answer.

It cost the girl an enormous effort to shove him off. But finally he rolled limply over. Yelling, the girl ran out into the living room. There was a long pause; finally sounds of movement from the other two bedrooms. The first to emerge was a naked male of middling age and somewhat paunchy appearance. Next, Bray came out with his shorts on. And then the two girls.

"Ssshh!" they said uneasily.

Maria hushed and explained that she had another dead man on her hands.

The five of them crowded into her tiny bedroom with her. It was Bray who, relieved, established that Kirk was still breathing.

"You'll have to call a doctor," the older male admonished, "but wait until my young friend and I have left."

Being a practical Diamondian, he clearly took the attitude that Bray and he were not involved in the matter. Whereupon he returned to the bedroom with his own girl, presumably completed the act for which he had paid her, dressed and departed.

Bray went down and phoned Struthers. The two men laboriously carried the body of Kirk down the four flights and into the station wagon and so back to the palace.

Once again the pretense of drunkenness got them past the lackadaisical door guards. They "walked" the limp body to Kirk's own room, used Kirk's key to get in, undressed him, and put him into bed.

"Whatcha gonna do with him?" asked the highly disturbed Struthers.

That, as Bray wearily explained, was a problem that he intended to confront with the coming of dawn.

"But we'll do something positive," he assured the older man.

Bray waited until the disconsolate Struthers had vanished into the distances of the hallway; then he himself emerged from Kirk's room. Since he still had Morton's keys, he now headed upstairs to Morton's bedroom. And it was there that he undressed and crawled deliciously into the splendid, large bed.

The previous night he had slept unthinkingly on the floor in his own room, having surrendered his bed to the unconscious Morton. Bray urged upon some doubting part of his

Self that remembering to come up to this magnificent room was a positive sign. It proved that he was in good enough shape and so had recovered from all that had happened. Yet even as he persuaded the reassuring thoughts to move through his mind, he was aware of a hollow feeling in the pit of his being; aware also of a continuing numbness that seemed to pervade his whole body.

He could guess emptily what the matter was. There was nothing to do; no way to turn; not a single thought that made real sense. The three possibilities that he did dredge up, as he lay there in old style Earth luxury, were not able to budge the doubts by more than a few inches: Marriott . . . the Diamondian peace committee . . . Lositeen—

Investigate Marriott (how was not clear), get some answers about the Diamondian peace group (that wouldn't be easy) . . . and find Lositeen, of course.

Sleep came somewhere in the wee hours and quieted all those jumpy neural impulses, while Bray caught a few blessed winks.

Meaning, he slept like a log.

Eighteen

MORNING, all too quickly.

Bray groaned himself out of bed, dressed and then checked on the two unconscious bodies. No change. In each case, Bray mentally predicted toilet disasters and thoughtfully inserted a thick, absorbent material both over and under each man's middle.

Best he could do for them.

He ate breakfast disconsolately. "Mrs. Bray," he said aloud to his faraway mother, "Diamondia is not the safest place for your darling."

On the way to his office a few minutes later, he realized belatedly that he had spoken to someone who was not present. Always, with him, a sure sign of inner perturbation.

He was sitting moodily at his desk, when the words of the great poem flitted through his mind. "They also serve who only stand and wait!" At once he addressed himself to the ancient poet: "It just doesn't feel as good, John."

He knew that he was waiting for something to happen, because he had no plan of his own. What could happen? He couldn't imagine.

The phone portion of his desk ViewComm rang suddenly. Bray jumped, then grabbed. The voice at the other end was Struthers. "Mr. Laurent's secretary wants to talk to Colonel Morton."

"Put him through to me," said Lieutenant Bray. He added under his breath, "Naturally."

The secretary to the ambassador extraordinary told Bray in a formal voice that the Earth federation forces had agreed to permit the latest Irsk prisoner to be interviewed by the head of Intelligence. He said, "This is an appointment that Colonel Morton asked for shortly after the Negotiating Committee arrived, and we have finally arranged it."

The appointment was for noon.

With one part of his mind, Bray heard himself explaining that Morton was expected to call in at any minute, and that of course he would be there to conduct the interview. With another part of his mind, he was trying to remember what he had heard of Morton's reasons for wanting to talk to an Irsk prisoner.

Not that it mattered. *"This is it,"* he thought. *"This is what I've been waiting for."*

He restrained his excitement as the secretary said in a severe, reminding tone: "They're expecting Colonel Morton himself. No one else. Make that very clear to your commanding officer."

"He'll be here," said Bray. And then he added, automatically, "God willing."

Bray decided to go alone.

A few minutes later, full of going forward juices once more, he paused beside Struthers' desk and explained carefully that somebody had better remain at the door of Morton's office and keep track of and an eye on and be a barrier, too.

"What about that positive action in connection with Mr. Kirk?" Struthers asked. *"And* the colonel."

It was a problem Bray still wanted to avoid.

"Some time today," he said vaguely.

As Struthers nodded glumly, the young officer walked firmly down the hall to Morton's private bathroom. Behind the locked door he performed the fateful operation upon his uniform. He had previously removed his own epaulettes and then put them on again with a double stick cloth. Now he peeled off his lieutenant's insignia and stuck on in their place the identification he had taken from Morton's uniform.

The transformation completed, he paused to gaze for a shuddery moment into the mirror. The face that stared back at him was lean, tanned, handsome and seemed to be, Bray hoped, its full twenty-two years of age.

He grew philosophical. What could happen if he were found out? It was difficult to imagine the Negotiating Committee stirring enough out of its lethargy even to take notice.

The realization buoyed him.

He was slightly surprised to find Struthers waiting for him in the hall. Struthers said in a sotto voice, "There's a Diamondian professor here to see Colonel Morton. He says he has an appointment."

"A Diamondian?" Bray echoed.

Struthers held up a desk calendar and pointed.

Bray glanced at his watch: 10:15. The name on the calendar opposite that hour was Professor Luigi Pocatelli. Under it was written in Morton's handwriting: "Familiar with Matters Irsk."

Bray shrugged. Actually, he had plenty of time. And it was a something and not a nothing. "Send him into the colonel's office. I'll come in by the other door."

Professor Pocatelli was a small, sandy haired, broad-faced, and smiling Diamondian. What he was smiling about quickly become clear; for, as Bray closed the door, he took an Earth federation hand grenade out of his coat pocket and said in a tense voice, but without losing his smile, "You will accompany me, or I will pull the cap of this grenade and that will be the end of both of us. As for me," he continued in an increasingly dramatic tone, "I shall die happy, knowing that I have given my life for the Diamondian people. As for you—" He paused.

Little curlicues of fear thoughts were angling through Bray. He did a kind of mental gulp and, in a manner of speaking, psychically coughed up an emotional equivalent of stomach juices and, finally observed with fascination a mind twist that said to him: Every day we lose three members of the Negotiating Committee—and I'm going to be one of today's three.

The feeling of shock continued. But the act of observing the exact fear unfroze him ever so little.

He began to think of what he might do.

Nineteen

THERE HE STOOD in Morton's gleaming office, with its kingly desk, the glittering, carved ceiling, the almost unearthly beauty of the decorated window alcove beside the desk and the stately door that led to the hallway where Struthers and a whole group of people were set up as, respectively, secretary and office help.

Standing on the far side of the desk was the stocky Diamondian dressed in a blue suit, from the coat pocket of which he had just pulled the gray and brown knobby object which was instantly recognizable for what it was to anyone who had ever seen one.

Another fleeting thought moved through Bray's mind. He remembered what the lower level Committee aide, Kirk, had said about both the Diamondians and the Irsk quickly finding out if they ever started phoning about Lositeen.

Similar reasoning obviously applied to Diamondians and (presumably) Irsk who were asked to visit members of the Negotiating Committee.

Here in New Naples a vast number of interested people would somehow find out about such a projected meeting, and then it would become a situation to scheme about. How to take advantage of a known appointment. A person who had achieved a penetration into the inner sanctum of an organization like the Negotiating Committee would be a valuable item. Knowing the time and the person, schemers and murderers could consider how they might take advantage.

Bray's mind jumped to the prostitutes, who in increasing numbers were entering the palace every night.

We are practically, he thought, amazed, *in a sieve.*

The instants that these thoughts and awarenesses required passed.

The shock faded.

He began to do and say necessary things.

With his captor's permission, Bray poked his head out of the main door and said to Struthers, "The professor and I are going out, and I'll see you later."

If the sergeant was surprised, it didn't show. "May I ask, sir," he said, "where you will be?"

"I'm going to see some exhibits," said Bray glibly, "and I'll call you from there."

"Very good, sir."

In the corridor, walking along beside a dangerously smiling Diamondian, who kept one hand in a coat pocket, (presumably still ready to pull the grenade cap) Bray silently conducted an experiment.

"All you ESP fans," he exhorted mentally, "that I keep running into in this building—" by this estimate fully fifty percent of the Negotiating Committee staff members were believers—"now is your chance to do a good practical turn for a colleague and prove your system."

As he telepathed his message, "It isn't exactly that I'm afraid of my luck running out," he thought. "But it would be darned handy in a pinch to know that somebody knew where I was and could rescue me in case of any emergency."

In the long magnificent corridors of this oversized version of the original Earth Palace by the sea, it appeared to Bray that nobody so much as glanced at himself and his—it seemed to Bray—highly noticeable companion.

Professor Pocatelli was visibly in an overstimulated condition. His eyes were bright, large brown baubles reflecting a kind of moist sunlight. His mouth was slightly wet, and although the entire building was air-conditioned day and night, his face glistened with great blobs of sweat, and a veritable stream of the stuff trickled slowly down his forehead, like a slow Niagara pouring out of his hairline.

It was really something to take note of. But no one did.

Then they were outside. And it was Bray's turn to start sweating, as the near noon heat of Diamondia's "temperate" zone hit him from a cloudless sky. But he was directed by quick, awkward gestures to a small car, which was parked by the curb a block from the palace. The little car had a smoky-faced Diamondian sitting at the wheel, a somewhat younger man than Pocatelli. Without a word, this person pulled the seat down so that Bray could get into the rear of the car. The professor crawled into the back seat also. At once, the noisy but powerful motor started up, and they were on their way.

Except for the hidden hand grenade, what followed was simply another typical wild ride through the streets of New Naples. Bray, who was not too familiar with the great city anyway, soon lost track of directions. Resignedly, he settled back as the professor talked and realized presently that the subject of discourse, of all things, was the Irsk this and the Irsk that.

Bray perked up. For here was information that Morton might be interested in. Bray recalled the room with the closed door in Lositeen's house. "My question," he asked, "is what would have been inside?"

"His dead parents and other remote ancestors," Professor Pocatelli replied.

"You're kidding."

"No, you see, the Irsk believe that no Irsk ever really dies. So they preserve the husk, that is, the body. Most are kept hidden and apparently never moved. But we have reports of people meeting some of these empty shells wandering around in the forests. There must be billions of them, but where most of them are kept we do not know."

Bray closed his eyes and tried to convert the living-dead concept into energy phenomenonology. It was hard for him because the after death world was one which he had rejected early. He could imagine, however, that the Catholic Diamondians might well be strongly affected by such a metaphysic.

His practical mind leaped at once to the possibility that perhaps some energy manifestation peculiar to the Irsk was involved. Was it possible the Irsk had converted it to the spirit form for the benefit of the believing Diamondians?

Abruptly, Bray realized it was too big a subject for him to examine from the equivalent of an armchair in mad motion through the streets of New Naples. He opened his eyes and said, "I'd like to meet one or more of these husks. What are they supposed to be able to do?"

"Well, of course, they can kill," was the reply.

"What else?" said Bray wearily, dismissingly.

"But they have other powers as well," said the professor.

Even this level of conversation was suddenly boring to Bray. His opinion of the Irsk had gone down. It all sounded like a form of primitive superstition. And he was tired. Oh, lord, he was tired of simple minds.

Yet he had another thought. "All the Irsk," he asked, "who have been killed in the war—are they still alive, too?"

"Since we Diamondians," replied Luigi Pocatelli. "have burned the dead bodies, it's a fine point. The Irsk say, yes, they are still alive. But I would say these are pretty shadowy husks."

By the time these words were spoken, they were pulling up to the curb of a street in the "old" city. A long line of dirty shops, a littered sidewalk, an odorous, heated atmosphere, like breathing garbage that has had a chance to stench it up in direct sunlight, was the near view.

Every one of the Diamondians was talking. No one was listening.

That was the appearance.

The noise of the voices rose above the roar of the little, vicious cars.

Bray said, "There's no question in my mind. This whole Diamondian problem has somehow been caused by people being people. Human beings descended on this planet and impinged on the local condition. It has never been the same since."

"What are you saying," said Professor Pocatelli—he pointed to where he wanted Bray to go—"is, I hope, not a reflection on the Diamondian people."

"Not at all." Truthfully, "I love the Diamondians. Everybody does. This is why we're all so concerned. What to do?"

"This way!" The professor motioned toward a gate that led into the yard of a small castle, adding, "Because of this love you feel and this concern, Colonel Morton, we must definitely keep the intense young men under control in your presence."

Definitely, thought Bray.

That proved impossible.

As they entered a large room, a dozen Diamondians of various ages stood up.

Three were men who had been at the Ferraris farm two nights before, with Marriott—young men who glared at Bray, recognition in their every aspect.

When the uproar died down, Professor Pocatelli was a ruined man, a fool who had let a "boy" pass himself off as a colonel.

By this time a gun was pointing at Bray, and the hour of reckoning was upon him.

What convinced Bray was the look on Professor Pocatelli's face. A give up expression of disaster. In an odd way, the man who had so dramatically captured him in Morton's office had been, for several minutes, on his side.

The look on the broad face abandoned the erstwhile captive. Pocatelli turned away with a grievous shrug—and Bray said hastily, "Gentlemen, before you do anything irrevocable, let me tell you this whole story."

The thin-faced killer with the gun relaxed ever so slightly. Suddenly he seemed less drawn together at the shoulders.

And, at a nod from the man called Mark, he slipped his pistol back into his pocket.

"What we're most interested in," said Mark softly, "is what happened to Isolina. But we welcome all information."

Bray did not dissemble. It was half-past truth time, with not a minute to spare. To these Diamondians murdering somebody was not a problem that they had to resolve with their consciences.

He talked with almost no reservation. He told them of the blackness in Morton's brain and his own. Told them of the mind switch that Morton had experienced.

One of his reservations was that he did not name Lositeen. That information was too precious, and besides he sensed it was not necessary. He described how the Irsk had spared Morton because they called him a "mind" brother, and that they had spared Isolina because they had somehow gotten the mistaken belief that she was Morton's girl friend.

He described Morton's second unconsciousness and where the body was now.

As he told the improbable tale, Bray progressively and anxiously wondered if these men would really believe what he was telling them.

Abruptly he was interrupted. "Ferdinand, get the station wagon," Mark commanded.

"Yes, yes."

Ferdinand rushed off without a moment's wait, and Mark turned toward Bray again. His eyes were flushed with excitement. "We'll get Morton," he said. "We'll fly his body and join the new peace delegation with it, show him to the Irsk and demand an explanation."

"But—" protested Bray weakly.

He wanted to say, "But how are you going to get him out of my bedroom and through all those corridors? Getting him in was easy, because we said he was drunk."

He didn't say it.

Sitting there, tied in the chair, he had a sudden sinking feeling that they *would* get Morton's body.

The possibility that Morton would not be safe inside the guarded building of the Negotiating Committee's headquarters had simply not occurred to him during his time of confession.

All the color that had not previously departed now drained from Bray's face.

Kind of sickish—that was the feeling in his stomach region. He grew aware that somebody was untying his legs.

He stood up moments later on watery legs. Not too watery, because he was able to remain standing.

The room quivered a little in the way his eyes beheld it. Outside the heat seemed farther away, as if he were no longer quite that connected with his burning skin.

As it turned out—

All these quivery feelings were, in a way, justified. They did get in; nobody stopped them. A somewhat recovered Bray, however, made a substitution. Four Diamondians carried the stretcher with David Kirk's body on it out of Kirk's room, along a crowded corridor; and they stood waiting while Bray, with Mark and Ferdinand, signed him out. "We're taking him to the hospital," said Bray, glibly.

When the listless guards had gone through their automatic routine, Bray turned to Mark and said, "And now if you gentlemen will excuse me, I have to go."

Having spoken, he turned his back and, being of a judicious nature in such moments, he broke into an easy lope.

A minute later, as he paused for the elevator door to open, he allowed himself a glance back.

The little group of men with the stretcher had disappeared.

"Well," thought Bray, "well."

He headed for Morton's office, to Struthers. "Sergeant," he said, "call the federation people and tell them Colonel Morton was unavoidably delayed, but that he'll be over to talk to that Irsk prisoner by 1:30 for sure. And then phone Dr. Gerhardt and make an appointment for me, that is, for Colonel Morton, for . . . for 2:45. Tell him it's urgent."

He departed as hastily as he had spoken.

Twenty

As HE STEPPED outside, the heat hit him. Bray moaned softly. But he made it to the auto park without turning into a soggy lump.

He took Morton's decorated, air-conditioned car and drove in grand style to the Earth federation headquarters in the Palazzo Reale.

Like so many of the other old buildings that had been, so to speak "duplicated" in New Naples, the beautiful Palazzo

Reale, a relict of the Spanish occupation of old Italy, had been built about five times the size of the original.

Bray gulped down a mild uneasiness as he gave Morton's name through a small wicket. This was "enemy" country for a man, Morton, who only the night before had been ordered arrested by someone in this very building.

As he hopefully anticipated, the left hand, so to speak, of the Earth federation forces did not know what the right hand was doing. He was admitted without argument.

Bray stood in due time in one of the below ground levels in front of a closed door from inside of which came the sounds of struggle.

The noise ceased. Bray opened the door and saw pretty much what he had expected. The Irsk had been stuffed by main force into the glasslike cage opposite the interrogation table. The door of the cage was closed and locked, and all was smooth and hard and unbreakable inside, with not a single protuberance for a tentacle to fasten on to.

The soldiers, under the direction of a young and red-faced—from exertion, no doubt—lieutenant, retreated to the back of the room and there fell into step and marched out through the rear door, which they closed behind them.

When the Earth federation unit had gone, Bray spread his notes on the table before him and mentally reviewed the means by which he hoped to cajole the prisoner in the cage.

He was aware of the tensed eyes watching him with a kind of contempt. It was into those eyes that he suddenly lifted his own gaze.

"Please notice," he said, "that I'm not a Diamondian and not an Earth federation officer. I'm a member of the Negotiating Committee."

The expression on the Irsk's face changed to disgust. But the being made no comment.

"Nothing in what I'm about to say," continued Bray, "will in any way infringe upon your self-respect as a loyal Irsk."

The eye seemed more wary now and less critical. But still the Irsk said nothing.

"We know about the Lositeen Weapon," said Bray. "What we do with it will depend on whether or not you will agree to accompany me to meet Lositeen and hear from him that he intends to give us the planetary weapon, so that you can report this fact to your top leader."

He paused, and now his casual eyeing of the others became a fixed stare. The Irsk stared back.

There was another long pause. "Then: "I have communicated to the merciless killers what you have just said," he answered.

Bray sat there. He couldn't speak. His lighthearted approach to life, normally a defense against reality, was penetrated. It was such a victory. In the two days since his capture this Irsk had refused to utter a single remark to his captors—not even a curse; total rejection of communication. The human being had to fight the jubilance that surged through him; tried not to indicate by so much as a narrowing of his eyes that he, also, was suddenly in a state of excitement.

Was his plan going to work? Would he find out what he wanted to know?

What bothered him was that in those two bits of information, the naming of Lositeen and of the weapon, he had used up everything he knew for sure on that subject. Oh, he knew, of course, that Lositeen lived in a small village. And he knew that Lositeen worked in a hardware store and lived in a two-story Irsk house about eight minutes walk west of the store. And that in the near background was a range of mountains. These things only Morton had noticed. Absolutely nothing more.

Bray braced himself, and his brain poured forth a tense thought: Say something. Make a personal response. Name the village because you take it for granted that I know where Lositeen lives.

The Irsk was making a dismissing gesture with one of his tentacles. He said, "I'm surprised that you're prepared to give the time to a trip into the southern mountains, but the merciless killers are willing for me to make the journey. They have just tried to contact Lositeen, but as usual he refuses to receive messages from the fighters; and they would like to find out through me if what you said is so."

He finished casually, "As a prisoner I, of course, have nothing but time . . . until the Diamondians get me away from you and execute me."

"The Diamondians are not going to get you," said Bray.

The contempt was back in the other's eyes. "You don't know these Diamondians like we do," was the reply. "The Negotiating Committee is not aware of the way prisoners disappear from the Earth federation prisons and show up for a few minutes in front of Diamondian firing squads."

It was an aspect of life on the planet that Bray had tried not to know about. Was it really going on? If so, it would be the work of collaborators at top officer level.

With a bracing of his shoulders, arms, chest and stomach area, he contained the strong feeling that came upon him as he had these thoughts. Later for that.

Aloud, he said, "What is your name?"

"We all have instructions not to give our names," said the dyl. But he spoke reluctantly.

"This is a special situation," urged Bray. "It may be late afternoon before we start, and if I know your name, I can make sure that you at least are not spirited away during that time."

There was a pause. Then: "My name is . . . Zoolanyt."

It was the moment of decision. Bray reached for the button on the desk in front of him.

He couldn't bring himself to push it.

They'll let him be killed, he thought.

He stood up. "You'd better come with me," he decided. "Right now."

He glanced at his watch. "I have another appointment," he said.

Bravely he walked down to the cage. Without pausing, he released the catch and swung the door open. He did step back, but only a few feet, as Zoolanyt emerged.

"We'll have to get me a green-striped shirt quickly," said the Irsk, "so I can look like a Friend of the Diamondians."

"I'll leave you in the car," said Bray in a steady voice, "and go into a store and buy you one. What's your size?"

By the time those words were spoken, they were out in the corridor, walking rapidly toward the stairway that would take them up and out.

What followed was slighly incredible to Bray, but it happened exactly as he had said it. He did leave Zoolanyt crouching in the car while he went into a store and bought one each of a green-striped coat and shirt. And when he came out there still was the car with the Irsk in it. The creature hastily donned both the shirt and the coat and then settled back with a sigh of content into the front seat beside Bray.

"That feels a lot better," he said. "Where to now?"

"I have to see a psychiatrist about something." Bray said, "and I'll have to leave you in the car while I go talk to him."

"Is it all right," asked Zoolanyt, "if I turn off the air conditioning while you're with him?"

It was all right with Bray all right.

Twenty-One

"COLONEL," the young psychiatrist's tone was diplomatic as he addressed Bray. "I'm willing to write down on this sheet that you've been overworking, and that you could use a rest at the base hospital on Sirius B-12."

He was a long, gangling type, and he sat behind a desk with that strange look of a small, youthful face hidden behind the dark rims of oversized spectacles.

He bent forward now and placed his pen in a position for writing. "Is that all right with you?" he asked.

As if it were only a matter of form, as if he took it for granted that any man on active duty would acquiesce instantly, or—which Bray considered more likely—as if he had been in communication with the part of Earth federation headquarters that knew about Morton's arrest and had received instructions to do what he was now proposing, the pen in his hand actually started to move.

At that point, Bray said, "Absolutely not."

The moving pen jerked a little and then lifted clear of the paper. A surprised, youthful face stared up at Bray. "What?" The young man swallowed hard, and then he stiffened. "It is my judgement," he began formally, "that—"

Bray stood up. And now he reached forward, took hold of the paper, and as the psychiatrist grabbed for it, jerked it away from him. And then, easily holding the other off with one arm, he held him there, while the man flailed with both his arms and uttered threats that Bray didn't hear because he was reading the document.

It was typewritten, and it stated briefly the things that the young doctor had spoken out loud. It had only been his signature that he had started to write when Bray's reaction stopped him.

"Well, well," said Bray. "Got it all down here on the basis of what I said on the phone. If all your judgements are delivered like this at long distance, without examination, I may feel compelled to recommend that you be sent back to rehab for retraining in some other less demanding occupation." He broke off. "Now will you sit down there and listen?"

The flailing ceased. A sly look came into the young man's

eyes. His gaze flicked to the door then over to the buzzer, as if he were sizing up his chances of contacting assistance.

Nothing in his manner indicated that Bray's right to a fair hearing had penetrated, yet, with an elaborate show of being relaxed, he sat down, and he even managed a fixed smile as he watched Bray tear up the "disposition of personnel" sheet and drop the pieces onto the desk.

Bray also sat down, but he remained straight up and alert, gazing uneasily at the psychotic in front of him—for what was a stereotyped determination to do violence to another person (no matter at whose request) but precisely psychosis? Somehow he had to penetrate that barrier of preconception, prejudgement and self-protective routine, which showed in the way the other man held himself, in his face, in his eyes and the curl of his lips.

He had, it seemed to Bray, to convey one message to this man's brain. Somehow Bray must let him know that his genuine knowledge, if it could be separated from his madness, was badly needed.

First make one more try for the assistance without the threat.

"Doctor," Bray said, "can you do hypnosis?"

The face before him grew tolerant, superior. The young man said in a pitying tone, "I'm sorry. I can't recommend hypnosis for you—"

The young doctor, it seemed to the unhappy Bray, was clearly not yet listening with his training but only with his instructions.

I'll have to fight to make it out of this building, Bray thought. It would be a battle between unsubtle psychiatric gadgets and the Intelligence equipment which he had—reluctantly—reinstalled in his uniform that morning.

He presumed, sadly, that professional pride would make it impossible for Gerhardt to let himself be outmaneuvered. So he must be ready for emergencies or confrontations with dangerous types such as a fraudulent Colonel Morton.

No alternative.

Bray made the first move in what he believed would be a rapid battle. He had had his hand out of sight, close to his service automatic. Now he drew that weapon and brought it into view above the level of the desk. "Doctor, I want you to accompany me to a little village in the southwest mountains, where you will hypnotize an Irsk. You can either come along because you're tired of inaction, or you can come along as

99

my prisoner. You tell me which and we'll go along from there."

He got an unexpected reaction. The face of the young man in front of him turned a sickly white.

Fear!

Bray was astounded. Could it be that Gerhardt was so new that he had never seen action before?

It seemed to be so. Here was a naïve villain; so much so that his first countermove was almost a joke, it was so transparent. Suddenly color came back into the cheeks. He grew brisk. He said, "I'll have to get my hypnotic equipment."

Later, thought Bray condoningly, when he gets older, he won't give himself away with such an obvious reaction.

He stood by grimly while the hypno-gun was placed in its carrying case . . . and not used on Bray. Bray carried the case while the crestfallen Gerhardt preceded his captor out into the corridor.

They walked along the hallway of the hospital of the Sisters of Divine Mercy, with its numerous wounded. The young psychiatrist's face behind the thick glasses had a blotchy look.

The two men emerged onto the steps of the hospital and upon a scene that was totally Earthlike. In the immediate foreground were some of the dingiest buildings of the coastal heights. Beyond, around the curving shore were the white colonnades and the terraced gardens, dark green with foliage, rising like an amphitheater from the sea. The vine-covered heights of the Vomere, with its palaces and villas, and the crown effect of Mount Casmoldoli, with its convent spire, was a noble background in the distances to the left.

As usual, Bray had no time to more than glance at those magnificent evidences of Diamondian genius. He hurried his captive to where Morton's Committee car waited and urged Doctor Gerhardt into the rear seat.

It took a little time to gesture Zoolanyt out of the front seat and to whisper to him that he wanted to protect himself while he drove from any violence the medical man might be contemplating.

Not, Bray reflected as he drove, that he really thought there was much murder in Dr Gerhardt. That young villain could strike underhanded blows at the sick and the trapped, but Gerhardt was not yet up to the level of a genuine confrontation with a determined opponent.

Later perhaps. Bray had a great faith in ultimate human courage, but it needed to be drawn out.

He intended to try to draw it out of the young doctor.

Back to the Negotiating Committee palace, up an elevator to the roof—and there was the plane that he had ordered in the name of Colonel Morton.

He motioned Zoolanyt into the pilot's seat. "Once up in the air," he said, "I'm not sure that I could trust you. So you'd better be pilot—I presume you can fly."

It was a fairly ridiculous question. Centuries ago the arriving human beings had found a sky-oriented Irsk culture. The beings had tiny little machines that flew—for an Irsk. Nobody else could get them to move. When asked about it, the good-natured natives pointed at their own heads with an offhand movement of a tentacle, and said, "It takes the brain, too."

These human-built machines were mechanically driven by a combination of antigravity and propellant system. But Bray was not surprised when the Irsk made the familiar, casual of course, gesture with his body, and said, "Yes."

They settled into the machine, with Gerhardt and Bray in the rear seat and Zoolanyt up front. At which point, Bray went on. "The map of the southern mountains is up there above the forward viewplate. That little red spot is us. It will move as we move, and so you can watch your progress. Or would you like additional directions?"

The Irsk was leaning forward. "Hmmm," he said. He placed the point of one tentacle on a spot that Bray couldn't make out in detail from where he sat, but he could see *about* where it was. "Right here," said the Irsk—and still he didn't name the village (but it didn't matter now; it was too late)—"so if we follow a north-northeast route, we'll just about hit it."

Bray dared not say a word. He was both jubilant and ashamed of himself. For it was this naïve quality in the Irsk that had made them so vulnerable to the commercially minded Diamondians. And now he was doing it to an Irsk, also. But for a good cause, he told himself.

A moment after that they were airborne; and he did with that guilt—and with the guilt about Kirk—what he always had in similar situations; pushed it into a corner of his mind which he had long ago labeled—psychiatric department, repository for future disasters of an emotional nature.

Over three small monutain ranges and down into a village square . . . twenty-eight minutes of rapid flight.

Slightly less than 200 miles, Bray estimated.

So it was still afternoon. In fact, as he stepped to the

ground, Bray glanced at his watch and instantly felt the excitement of triumph. "Lositeen," he said, "is probably still on the job."

The other two passengers were stirring. Dr. Gerhardt's bespectacled head poked out the door. "You want me now?" he asked.

Bray said he did and simultaneously motioned the Irsk to remain in the pilot's seat. After the gangling psychiatrist had extricated himself from the tiny interior, Bray peered inside and said to Zoolanyt, "I notice the hardware store just down the street. You remain in the plane. I want only Dr. Gerhardt to accompany me on this first phase."

The Irsk seemed disconcerted. He had clearly expected to accompany Bray to the initial confrontation with Lositeen, and so apparently had his remote contacts—"the merciless killers"—for there was a pause; and then, "You're leaving me in charge of the plane?"

It was exactly the thought and awareness that Bray wanted the other to have. Alone inside the aircraft, he would feel secure because theoretically he could escape if he wished. Experience had shown that such dilemmas were too much for an Irsk. He would, Bray hoped, sit there like a hypnotized chicken.

Zoolanyt called doubtfully, "You'll bring him over here?"

"Of course," said Bray.

And there they were, walking without a backward glance across the simulated cobblestone street. The cobbled effect was visible through a transparent, smooth surface that was tough but bouncy. Easy to walk on, no skidding, looking like the original but with modern safety effect.

The little town, still unnamed, resembled some of the pretty villages Bray had seen on his inspection flights as Morton's aide; but he didn't specifically remember having been in this one. Several passersby had paused to watch the plane land. But it was evidently not that uncommon a sight; as the two men approached, all turned away with the faint, faraway looks of people who have better things to do.

To the west, as he walked, Bray saw that the shadows lay long below the mountain wall. From right there (he thought) the Irsk fighters came down and intercepted Lositeen on this very street, while simultaneously Morton was somehow perceptually inside him watching and hearing everything. Fantastic.

Bray's thought ended. Because there was a faint sound from his companion. He glanced around hastily and then stopped. Gerhardt had come to a halt and was standing several feet away. There was a stubborn expression on his face.

"Not one step farther," said the voice from under the big glasses, "until I know what this is all about."

"Oh!" said Bray, "of course."

He had been, he realized, inconsiderate. He extended the little satchel which contained the hypno-gun and explained in a voice that was intended to appease exactly what he wanted. Gerhardt's expression remained unhappy and anxious. So Bray hastily finished, "Requires no bravery. I'll distract his attention, and you shoot him in the back."

For bare moments after he had explained in that blunt fashion, Bray had a qualm. As if he had made the deed sound too villainous. But a swift second glance at the psychiatrist reassured him. Gerhardt suddenly had a brighter look to him. He straightened. He said in a voice that only trembled slightly, "You can count on me, colonel."

Clearly the method was exactly the limit of the young doctor's present capability. Bray left him outside, standing peering at the window of the hardware store. As he entered, he had not the slightest fear that he might be betrayed. Zoolanyt in charge of the plane, Gerhardt with no place to escape to immediately and probably aware that he was under the gaze of the Irsk—perfect.

Inside, Bray quickly examined a display of small items, selected one, and with it in his hand approached the desk at the rear. There were no humans in sight; which, so far as Bray was concerned, was exactly where every Diamondian wanted to be, workwise. A single Irsk clerk accepted his money and wrapped up his purchase. As the dyl handed him the package, Bray said, "May I ask your name?" He spoke politely.

It was Lositeen.

. . . It was six o'clock when Lositeen emerged from the door and headed for home. When he had walked a few dozen feet, Bray and Gerhardt stepped out from a door. Bray gestured at him unthreateningly. "We'd like to speak to you, Mr. Lositeen," he said courteously.

Lositeen stopped and waited politely. Bray introduced himself as Morton and said, "Unknown to you, the darkness lodged another person's self—I don't know how else to describe it—inside your mind. This was several days ago. We would like to discuss the matter with you."

Lositeen's manner had changed. "I," he said slowly, "have

just tried to communicate with the merciless killers and they refuse me contact. I reason from this that they don't want to interfere with your plan. My advice is, don't do anything hastily."

It was too late. As Bray talked, Gerhardt had casually taken up a position slightly behind Lositeen. From there, without pause and actually without listening to the conversation and possibly even being in too keyed up a condition to hear it, he fired the hypno-gun.

At and into Lositeen. And then, virtually without pausing, turned slightly and discharged an equal dosage at Bray.

The appearance of fear, Gerhardt was smiling to himself as he finally got his chance, often put people off guard just long enough.

The smile faded abruptly. A terrifying weakness all through his body . . . his legs would not support him. As he dazedly felt himself crumple to the sidewalk, he realized vaguely that something glittery, a tight beam of shining liquid or gas, had spurted up at him from Colonel Morton's uniform.

Unconsciousness blotted out his automatic tendency always to analyze what gas it might be.

— Twenty-Two

TIME HAD ALSO PASSED for David Kirk.

He lay in some kind of limbo. He could see nothing, but he could feel his body, or so it seemed.

He remembered quite clearly what had happened. There he had been in his favourite position atop an attractive female; which female had never mattered to Kirk. Maria, for his purposes, was as suitable as Marian. Suddenly, the wave of blackness had become bigger and stronger. Maria disappeared. And here he was in a vacuum.

Am I ill?

He spoke the question out loud or tried to. No sound came. All around him was total silence. And though he repeated the words, and others also a few times, nothing happened. So presently he shrugged and lay there, waiting.

How much time went by, he had no idea. Hours? Days? It was impossible to guess. The question of how long it would

104

go on was, however, resolved suddenly. A baritone voice said to him, "Have you come to a decision?"

The words were spoken quite close to Kirk's ears. They appeared, therefore, to be directed at him. Decision? he thought. About what? . . . Brief bafflement. Even a tiny impulse to be naïve and ask what was the meaning of all this.

Naturally, being David Kirk, he was incapable of such a faux pas. As soon as he could, after a few seconds only, after he had time to realize that it could be that somebody had actually heard his own voice earlier and that conversation was possible, he said cautiously, "Would you outline for me again exactly what I am to make a decision about?"

The baritone voice explained, "I must have your agreement that you will help me exterminate the Diamondian people."

"Of course, I will," said David Kirk. "So what's next?"

Twenty-Three

AT THE SAME INSTANT that those accepting words were spoken, Morton woke up in a strange bedroom.

Lying there in the bed, staring up at an unfamiliar ceiling an appalled feeling came over him. He was free . . . but he had a memory of having agreed to help the darkness wipe out the Diamondian people.

That, he argued with himself, is ridiculous. I could never have done such a thing. Nevertheless, as he climbed off the bed, he noticed his body was doing the positive feedback tremble, his long time signal from inside his skin that he had done something he shouldn't have done. Could it be, could it be that he had agreed because it was the only way to get away from the monster that had held him prisoner?

Suddenly he was confused. Because his memory of his agreement seemed to include that reality, also.

What bothered him was that there would undoubtedly come a moment when the darkness would realize that he intended to renege. What then?

By the time he had that thought, Morton was over at the bureau looking at letters, identifying Bray's room. Relief. Implications fairly obvious. Brought from that sidewalk. Kept hidden. So no one knew. Good old Bray, he thought gratefully.

He found his uniform—and noticed the epaulettes were missing. As soon as he was dressed, he went up to his own apartment vaguely surprised to find himself thinking about David Kirk. It was a recognition name for him but no more. He recalled that Paul Laurent had an aide whose name was David Kirk.

Odd!

Was that part of the puzzle?

If it was, it would eventually be explained.

As he studied his pale face and drawn cheeks in the mirror of his bathroom, he thought of Paul Laurent several times. Which, except for the repetition, was reasonable enough.

He phoned the ambassador's office, made an appointment for eleven o'clock and then, ravenously hungry, went down to eat.

The time was a few minutes after eight o'clock.

Because of his rank he had access to the private commissary overlooking the ocean itself. And so he sat at a window table waiting to be served and gazed out across a misty sea to where on a clear day Sorrento was visible on the distant, curving shore.

As he ate breakfast, he peered down at the warm sea below. The ocean was doing its best to provide a steady tidal effect. Since Diamondia's moon was considerably larger than Earth's, the waters were moving in colossal surges; and the sound of that motion came up like the uneven thunder of big guns operating under the general order to fire when ready, kind of overwhelming.

Nonetheless, the monstrous sound soothed rather than troubled him. He had the feeling that in some quiet corner he would start to think — and would, of course, go mad in a few minutes.

... It was not an ocean, Morton reflected with a wry smile, for small craft. And, in fact, he had heard that big ships had their problems, also; like operating in an unending middle-sized storm.

Morton walked along corridors across beautiful gardenlike patios, heading toward the rear of the gigantic complex of buildings that made up the palace. His own office and quarters were as far from the ocean as he had been able to manage it.

Gradually the huge sound of the waves faded behind many walls. Slowly, as he realized that, a wan smile broke the gloom of his face. He couldn't help but remember with a faint pleasure how delighted everybody had been for him to have these

106

rear rooms. During the turmoil of arrival a few weeks before, the upper echelon people of the Negotiating Committee had fought a silent battle for bedrooms. Those who won got a sea view. For them, the nightmare began. For him—

As Morton entered his department, he could hear a faint clacking of computers and muffled voices from various rooms. But otherwise a heavenly silence.

He nodded a cheerful hello to his secretary, Sergeant Struthers, who gulped something in reply. A moment later Morton was past him and into his private office. Inside he sank into his comfortable chair, and his first act was to fumble through the mail and reports that lay on his desk. Thus he came upon the two items requested in his name by Bray.

The interview with Joaquin was particularly fascinating. When stopped, the Diamondian delegate survivor of the first peace group was handled so swiftly that he never even realized that he was under hypnosis and afterward remembered nothing.

And so here was that whole disgraceful story, and the role played by Joaquin in every phase of it.

The interrogating officer, Sutter, noted in his summary that Joaquin had "some hallucinations" while in the jungle. These were not described. Morton picked up his interoffice phone and called the officer.

Sutter entered in his fashion and accepted the chair that Morton motioned him to. His blue eyes reflected disbelief. "Colonel, you're not seriously suggesting we should spend time on the details of somebody's fantasies while suffering from shock. That's for the medical department."

Morton wasted no time. "Do you have any idea of the nature of the words spoken to Joaquin by the luminous figure that he, uh, fantasied?" To that he got the expected answer of no, and he immediately asked, "Where is Joaquin now?"

"We followed the routine. He believes he was held up for medical treatment. He was released last night. He expressed his intention of starting out for his home and planned to leave early this morning."

"Where's his home?"

"New Rome." In the silence that followed Sutter must have had his first qualms, for he said, "We could have somebody waiting for him when he arrives and fly him back here."

"About when would that be?"

"Well . . . it usually takes about a day to drive from New Naples to New Rome."

He concluded in a brave tone. "Pick him up at midnight or thereabout. Have him back here by four a.m. You could talk to him any time after that."

"Thank you, major," said Morton in an even voice. "Will you undertake to have Joaquin brought here?"

When Sutter had departed, Morton sat for a long moment, shaking his head in renewed wonderment. Oh, modern logic, he thought almost invocationally, if only your set theory were true. Everything would be so simple.

But unfortunately (with a sigh) the universe and all life operated on the infinitely differentiating reality of finite logic. Accordingly his chance of seeing Joaquin in time for it to do any good was slim. The information that could have been so easily obtained from one man, he himself would now have to get with difficulty before this day was many more hours gone.

With that realization he dismissed Sutter from the forefront of his mind and picked up Luftelet's report. It was a little sketchy for his requirements. Since he planned to visit Capodochino Corapo by one p.m. (and have a showdown with Marriott) he picked up the interoffice line receiver again and called Luftelet.

The major was also at his desk and came shuffling in a few minutes later. He settled into the chair beside Morton's desk with a resigned air.

Morton, intent on his own purpose, waggled one hand in a welcoming gesture and murmured good morning, while with the other hand he held Luftelet's report. Without looking up, he said, "I notice you refer here to the potentialities of the Corapo military post to build an intense magnetic field, but you don't give the figure in gammas. Do you recall, offhand?"

He stopped. Out of the corner of his alert eyes, he caught the body movement of his visitor. It was an all over gesture of resistance to the question. Surprised, Morton looked up at the man; and for the first time recalled with an inward sigh who this was.

The major was gazing at him, and his body and face were braced defensively. The whole truth of Luftelet cried out in that posture for the triumph of reason and honesty as against the pretense and presumption of lesser individuals.

Morton's hesitation was momentary only. He asked, "What is the figure?"

Luftelet braced himself even more and said, "Colonel, I respectfully submit that the report as I have prepared it, is exactly as it should be for anyone other than a person with my own technical qualifications. I—"

He faltered at that point, for there was something, a look, in the face of his superior that he had never seen there before.

The actual feeling in Morton was a sense of frustration, which derived from David Kirk's total disregard for the rights of people less fortunate than he was. What Morton reacted to was that at this critical moment, when every second might well be decisive, *this* creature had persisted with his monstrous stereotype.

In a single compression of tension the frustration generated an explosion. All these hours he had been subjected to stress and to one defeat after another; and in the entire series of disasters he had not once had a chance to fight the enemy. His muscles, which were always set to go toward situations rather than away from them, had been held in one timeless stasis after another. That latent impulse to reach forward had as a result intensified to where it was a hit back feeling.

All in a moment the civilized finite logic trainings that normally held him courteous, generous and almost completely nonviolent were overwhelmed. He was in the modern logic rage, and he did something he had never done before. He struck a subordinate.

He lunged from his chair almost as if he were catapulted. He bridged the three feet that separated him from Luftelet and landed one hard blow directly on that rigid jaw.

The leap forward, the irresistible strength, the blow itself became a single, continuous motion. In a way, then, Luftelet disappeared. His chair simply crashed over backward, and he with it.

The thick rug took the impact from the chair almost without a sound. The major was briefly unconscious and had not even the opportunity to yelp. By the time Luftelet came to, a startled (at himself) but not repentant Morton reached down and pulled the other man, chair and all, to an upright position again.

Morton turned and with a single, sweeping reach of his free arm grabbed Luftelet's report, held it in front of his eyes, leafed through it and said from between clenched teeth, "Where are the magnets anchored? What is their field strength exactly? And what is the formula on this? And the purpose of that group of molecular circuits?"

At his first spat out question he got a cringing reply; at his second a kind of half-shamed reply; at his third a reluctant answer; and his fourth question produced a response, but Major Luftelet was unquestionably coming to, for he added, "Colonel, I protest this—"

Morton's fifth question was, "And what is the finite logic number?" Luftelet's reply was, "It's 138,000." And that left Morton speechless.

So he came to the end of his questioning by two routes: the overwhelming effect of the vast number he had been given; and his sudden awareness that he was about to meet serious resistance to further interrogation. Without another word he grabbed Luftelet by the collar of his uniform, swung him out of his chair and, with that same effortless strength, toward the door.

As he opened it, he said, "Be ready by about 12 o'clock to accompany me to that building in Corapo. It will not be necessary for you to apologize for your behavior."

"Really, sir, it's your behavior that—" Luftelet must have seen the look in Morton's eyes. For he gulped and said, "I'll be ready." As Morton released him, the man half walked, half staggered past Struthers and so out through another door, and was gone.

Morton stepped out, also, and paused beside Struthers' desk. "Where's Lieutenant Bray?" he asked.

It was too soon for Struthers to tell the whole truth. He felt a desperate need to have a discussion with Bray before he incriminated the young officer. As a result he felt a great confusion.

"He hasn't come in today, sir," Struthers managed to say, truthfully.

Morton nodded almost absently. "I noticed," he said, "from a note on my desk that Bray acted in my name on several matters. So I think I'd better go down the hall and get a printout on what else he did. When he comes in, tell him I want to talk to him."

As he turned away, he added, "And tell one of the big ships to stand by for me starting in about ten minutes."

"Very well, sir."

In studying the printout a few minutes later, he was delighted to see that the machine had picked up several long conversations. He read them at high speed and wrote down the names: Professor Pocatelli and Mark, David, Kirk and Zoolanyt and—"I'll be damned!"—Gerhardt. . . . His and Bray's insignia, with their molecular circuit microphones and transmitters, had listened in clear and loud.

Morton's gaze flicked down to a significant line. Noted that the aircraft tracer system had dutifully recorded the flight of

110

the machine which Bray, using the authority of Colonel Morton (by way of Sergeant Struthers), had requisitioned the day before. Morton wrote down the name of the little mountain valley village to which the craft had flown. A few minutes later Struthers called information for him and then contacted the hardware store there. Whereupon Morton came on the line and asked for Lositeen.

A Diamondian voice answered, and when Morton had identified himself, the voice said with strong emotion, "Lositeen has not come to work this morning, and there is reason to believe he has been a victim of foul play by the rebel Irsk."

There had been a witness, it seemed. The man, watching from a window, had got the whole thing somewhat mixed, but he did observe what happened after Gerhardt fell down unconscious beside the bodies of Bray and Lositeen; the details of which had not been clearly recorded since no words were spoken.

The aircraft, guided by Zoolanyt, rolled swiftly across the street. The green-striped Irsk inside emerged hastily from its interior. He dragged all three bodies into the machine and climbed after them. Moments later the plane took off from the little village square.

Belatedly the witness advised the local Diamondian-military post. But a subsequent sky search failed to locate the machine with its four occupants.

Morton thanked his informant and hung up. A further study of the printout revealed that the aircraft was stationary—therefore landed—at one edge of the Gyuma Ravine.

You can only help people so much, thought Morton, grayly. What could he do for the lighthearted Bray at such a distance? For some hours, still, nothing.

He was uneasy. The feel of the final crisis was coming in from every side.

He sat there, hesitant about the thought he was having. Yet a truth pushed at him: *I may not have time to get back to this SRD room again....* So it was now or never for an insight which had made its first faint tracing in his mind when he realized that Bray had several times pretended to be Colonel Charles Morton, and David Kirk had been pretending to be Bray at the time that he became unconscious.

It occurred to him that the logic of his thought was literally black and white. If it was true, then he had to do what he was contemplating; and if it wasn't true, then a number of people would have an uneasy time of it for a few days.

111

In a crisis that can't be a barrier.

Hesitation ended.

He comm'd Dr. Jerome Fondier at the hospital for the Incuribili. As soon as the doctor identified himself, the SRD computer flowed an instant supersonic pattern along the open channel into the doctor's brain. The pattern seized control of the nerve mass in the brain stem. Fondier, under the consequent hypnosis gave Morton two names. One was that of the Earth federation officer who had actually issued the order for Morton's arrest. And the other was the name of the M.D. who had used the unconsciousness-inducing injection on Morton.

Morton ordered Fondier to: "Resign your hospital job, set up an office in a poor district and devote yourself to giving medical services to poor people at a low cost." He finished, "Do this under the name—listen carefully!—of Colonel Charles Morton."

He broke the connection feeling not at all regretful. There ought to be a number of Diamondians in the Morton lineup. The democratic idea required a broad base of viewpoints. And who better of the patriots than Fondier?

He gave the same command to the other doctor, whose name was Louis Gaviota. To the Earth federation officer, a Colonel Exeter, he said, "You will for five days insist that you are Colonel Charles Morton. Where that takes you I leave to the judgement of your associates."

His final act in the SRD room was a general order to the computer, which greatly expanded the number of Colonel Charles Mortons. He specified: "Select twenty-five hundred Diamondian males from all walks of life and an equal number of Earth federation men of all ranks below colonel and also select five thousand prostitutes. Choose half of these men and women from right here in New Naples and find the rest in widely separated parts of Diamondia. Tell all of these people that they will have a temporary identity problem, a strong conviction that their real name is Colonel Charles Morton. They will not reveal to anyone that they have this problem, but it will be a severe internal struggle."

He concluded: "To cancel all this, tell each individual he can phone the SRD—give him or her the necessary information—beginning five days from now. At that time you will dehypnotize the person and he will resume his own identity."

Normally the wartime powers of an on the spot Intelligence chief like himself operated no higher than on men with the rank of major, and even that was instantly reported by

Star-Transit to distant computers. By speaking a certain code word, he could extend his power to higher echelon officers, but such usage really set off alarm systems in distant key places. He had used that code word in order to include Colonel Exeter; in due course explanations would be required of him. A board of review would sit.

What bothered Morton was that he could think of no way by which Isolina might be included in the Colonel Morton circuit.

The computer comm'd all possible places where she might be, and everywhere met the same answer: not available.

Too bad.

Twenty-Four

MORTON CAME DOWN from the ship into the village of Nucea; stood on the ground; felt firmness of it beneath his own feet. And this time he gazed with his own eyes and perceived with his own senses.

The scene was sensationally familiar. Off to the left stood the Irsk village, with its dozens of bright gleaming colors and little spires attached to the houses. He sought automatically to locate Lositeen's two-story residence and found it almost right away. Even at a distance it looked real and solid. Not that it had been insubstantial before. Yet there was a difference, Morton realized. The difference was that with the passage of time his mind had diminished the reality of what he had seen through another living person's brain.

A few minutes to walk over. And there he was at the front door, the one he had expected Lositeen to enter that first evening.

The door opened.

The Irsk girl, who faced him a fleeting moment later, was the same as he had previously seen through Lositeen's eyes. The excitement came again, and he literally had to brace himself to do what he had to do.

He presumed she was already mentally advising the merciless killers of this visit.

Morton stood there on the doorstep of the Lositeen house and said quietly, "You are Ajeanantataseea?" He pronounced

113

the name in its Irsk fullness; ignored the short version: Ajanttsa.

She seemed taken aback by his knowledge of her identity. "You know me?" she asked in a trembling voice.

Morton reassured her. "Don't be alarmed," he said "I am not a Diamondian. I am a member of the Negotiating Committee."

"You are a human being," she said, "and I am an Irsk." Nonetheless, she seemed reassured. Her voice grew hostile. "Negotiation cannot solve that difference."

"Proper negotiation," said Morton firmly, "locates the real problem and solves that. Which is why I would like to look into that room."

Without waiting for her answer he stepped inside, forcing her slighter body to retreat. Leaving no room for doubt, he pointed across the hall to the door at which Lositeen had glanced so significantly that first night.

Once more—shock. "Oh, no," she gasped, "that's Lositeen's ancestral room." She pronounced the name by the long Irsk method: Leoosaeetueeeena.

"Is he here? Lositeen."

"No, he didn't come home last night."

Morton, who had his own reasons for believing that Lositeen was elsewhere, had not waited for her reply. He was already walking across that remarkable, gleaming floor. As she finished her statement, he took the final few steps and placed his palm over the curving latch. Then he glanced back at the female.

"My question," he said, "is who or what is in that closed room?"

The thin lips were parted with anxiety. "Lositeen's parents and other remoter ancestors," she said. She added earnestly, "What would you think of someone who entered your parents' tomb?"

"I understand these people are not dead as human beings understand death; and it my duty to see what that means." He spoke firmly, "And it is particularly important in connection with Lositeen, because he has the power to destroy the darkness."

The young female seemed overwhelmed by the extent of his information, for she said nothing more. Hastily Morton opened the door, walked in and closed it behind him.

For a while he simply stood there, just inside, gazing.

It was a large room, complete with drapes and carpets that did a considerable job of concealing the underlying Irsk iridescent wall, floor and ceiling material. Diamondian style furniture and a number of hidden light sources completed the decorative scheme.

Barely visible in the armchairs and on the settees were the Irsk . . . ghosts.

Luminous bodies sitting silent and unmoving. There were eight dyl and eleven adyl. Each male and female Irsk husk occupied a chair or part of a settee. What was eerie was that there they sat as still as death, and each figure was literally transparent.

The scene seemed out of a dreamworld. Yet Morton did not hesitate. He had a formulation as to what the existence of such transparent beings meant. So he walked to an empty chair and dragged it over in front of an older dyl. He settled himself into the chair.

Sitting there, he thought: It is my belief that that luminous figure in the jungle spoke to Joaquin and tried to get him to talk to it.

Therefore these creatures could communicate with human beings.

He said deliberately, "I am head of the Irsk government. I want to ask you some questions."

There was a long pause. Then the head turned very slowly. And the large, transparent eyes looked at him. The misty lips parted. No sound came, but a soft male voice spoke inside his head.

It said, "If you are in the circuit, then your duplicate will hear what I say and will transmit my words to you. . . ."

Morton closed the door of the "ancestral" room behind him and then stood staring at the Irsk girl. "What is the natural life span of an Irsk?" he asked.

The adyl was sullen. "It's well known," she replied, "that we live about five hundred Diamondian years."

Morton had heard the figure. But he was stubborn about where he got his facts.

And puzzled now. "That's a long life span," he said. "How would you explain such longevity?"

"We Irsk," she said, "had a perfect affinity with each other through the darkness. All that is endangered now. And something has to be done quickly. Recently Irsk have died as young as a hundred and thirty. Everybody is alarmed!"

"It could be the war," said Morton. "Maybe rebellion isn't good for people."

"It's better than slavery," she said acridly.

"History says the Irsk welcomed the first settlers and helped them."

"It didn't occur to those pure minds," the girl replied raspingly, "that their planet was going to be taken over."

Morton was a pragmatist. "It's happened—by whatever fashion. Now everyone has to learn to live with it."

"Impossible!" she flashed. She seemed to brace herself. "You were in there half an hour. What did you learn?"

"I learned," said Morton, following his straightforwardness rule, "that Lositeen's oldest, so to speak, 'living' ancestor duplicate is dear, old, pure Uteetenborasta, and that she is only fifth generation. Since the Irsk go back the usual billion or so years, how come ancestors only started with her?"

He added, "That's why I came. I had a feeling it was rather odd that a single room could contain the darkness duplicates of one Irsk's family tree."

He broke off. "The group in there only go back about two thousand years. What is your explanation?" he concluded.

"That's when the darkness came," she answered simply.

It was a possibility that had already occurred to Morton. Yet her confirmation startled him. Somebody had created this creature. . . . That's all we need, he thought, another great power, one capable of manufacturing a force as immense as that thing up there.

He braced himself, said, "Two more questions. First, why are they down here instead of up in the field where they belong?"

"When ten years ago my people finally rebelled against their Diamondian oppressors," she said sullenly, "many people like Lositeen, who did not rebel, brought their family duplicates away from the darkness, which might otherwise out of its own developing disturbances have damaged them."

"My second question," said Morton, "is where is the Lositeen Weapon?"

"It's with Lositeen's duplicate," she said calmly.

"You mean—in there?" Morton indicated the room from which he had just emerged. "I saw his duplicate just now."

"Of course not—" she began sharply. And stopped. Something in his tone must have been suddenly convincing. She spun away from him and glided to the door, shoving it open with a gesture of one tentacle.

She stood there. Had she been human, Morton would have sworn that the movement her body presently made was the swaying of someone on the verge of fainting.

116

But she controlled herself. She turned, closing the door as she did so. And she came back to him.

Morton said, "Can you speak to him? He wouldn't answer me."

"No, he doesn't accept messages."

Morton said, "If the Lositeen Weapon isn't with Lositeen's duplicate, where could it be?"

The girl had no idea. She seemed to be in shock. "I have a feeling," she said in a distracted tone, "that something terrible has happened. But I don't know what."

Morton, who had the same feeling, combined with the additonal realization that his time was running out, thanked her and departed.

Minutes later he stepped off onto the roof of the palace. It took almost as long to get down to his office as it had required to "fly" from Nucea to New Naples.

Twenty-Five

ELEVEN O'CLOCK. At last.

As he was admitted to the Presence, Morton was again reminded that only other lesser echelon types and his staff and he, who had those delightful rear quarters, could obtain a sound sleep in this seaside palace.

What reminded him was that the Very Important Person looked as if he could use a good night of shuteye. He kept rubbing his eyes.

Morton had been ushered in. The door closed behind him. There he stood waiting to be noticed by the individual behind the desk, who seemed to be studying a document after the manner of such people. Morton accepted the delay as a rare opportunity to evaluate the Great Man.

The face was long, very white and intelligent. (Distinguished was the word that flickered through Morton's mind.) The eyes were slightly narrowed, lips parted just a little, hair graying at the temples but mostly dark brown.

Morton on meeting him a few months earlier had estimated him to be in his early fifties. His name was Paul Laurent, and he was in origin, French.

He was the Earth federation ambassador extraordinary, head of the Negotiating Committee.

What had puzzled Morton at the time of his original introduction to the man, and what puzzled him again now, was the feeling: I've met this man before!

When? Where? And why was it difficult to recall an individual of such unusually distinctive appearance?

Once more the older man rubbed his eyes, and then he looked up at Morton and smiled in a friendly fashion. "Well, Charles," he said, "the high command wanted me to have along at least one man whose muscles moved him into situations rather than out of them. What have you been inclined to get into?"

The question was a small pebble tossed into the pool of memory of what Morton had been up to, but he avoided a direct answer.

He was here, among other things, to talk about Marriott. But he intended to approach that touchy subject indirectly.

"Your Excellency," he protested, "what really bothers me about what we're doing here is that there seems to be no plan. And why is it that except for the building over in Corapo we haven't brought our advanced weaponry onto this planet? The men surely guess, and their officers know, that they are being treated unfairly."

"Do you suggest," asked the older man in a neutral tone, "that Earth federation forces should have come in here and helped human beings to restore their hegemony?"

The question really hit at the core of the problem. Which was a little surprising. Morton hadn't expected such penetrating awareness from any member of the somnolent Negotiating Committee.

"Well, no!" he admitted.

"We have on this planet," Laurent continued, "a situation unique in Man's galaxy. The women's unions never made any converts here. Or if they did, it doesn't show. You see—" the older man broke off "—I have taken note of your reports on these matters."

It seemed a minor aspect, but Morton waited.

Laurent said, with a faint smile, "What has happened on Diamondia we owe to the supermasculinity of the magnificent Diamondian male, and it would be a little difficult to put that masculinity on trial."

Morton, who desired most urgently to get over to Capodochino Corapo, decided that he had better indicate—to save time—that he was familiar with the male-female anomalies of Diamondia. He did so succinctly. He also, after a hesitation, voiced his conviction that the Earth federation forces were

118

not—as they usually were—neutral but determined. They were fighting to restore order and to do justice to all parties according to Earth federation law in such matters. "My impression is, sir, that for some reason both officers and men have strongly taken the side of the Diamondian people in this war, and that, while it may be the policy of High Command on Arcturus IX to be fair to the aliens on this planet, this is not the attitude of the military forces now operating in the Diamondian theater."

All the time he spoke he was aware of the older man regarding him with a quizzical smile. When he had finished Laurent nodded.

Naturally (he said) there had been many repercussions from the war. Among others—and this was the answer to Morton's puzzlement about the bias of the Earth federation forces—millions of Diamondian girls converted overnight from obstructive amateur to hostile (but infinitely available) prostitution. And so Diamondia (said Laurent) was a male paradise. The arriving troops had found vast numbers of prostitutes available in all the cities where they were stationed. "And as you know, Charles, there are no fleshpots anywhere else. Elsewhere the women's unions have such a tight control that life has become a hell for men. We may surmise that Diamondian men never did allow civilization to make as many inroads on the women situation. And when the Irsk ceased doing all the labor, it forced an economic condition which overnight sent girls out into the street to make a living."

The ambassador extraordinary continued, "You'll have noticed that our own palace has taken on the appearance of a house of prostitution—"

The great man paused, as if anticipating comment. But Morton remained silent. He sensed that he had miscalculated, should not have interrupted earlier. There were sharp observations here. . . . Amazing how much Laurent, who had never to his knowledge left the palace, had observed.

"Charles, we owe you double for keeping you in ignorance as we have done. Our excuse has been that anyone who was in the open, as you were, might inadvertently have had his brains picked."

He paused. Then: "Charles, there's something special about the magnetic field around this planet."

The excitement that came to Morton in that moment was all the more intense because there had been no lead-up to such a revelation. All that small talk, and now, suddenly—

119

Incredibly they had got *that* far. Deep inside him a solitary hope curled open its life-seeking petals. Yet an overall uneasiness remained. . . . an intuition that Laurent's facts were twelve hours late.

"Fourteen years ago," said Laurent, "when the Diamondian situation began to puzzle High Command on Arcturus IX, we commissioned a young physicist to settle here with the purpose of investigating the magnetic field. During his entire study he has carried protective equipment. Ten years ago he was provided with a special protective building, a D.A.R., and given what seemed to be a small official job as head of the military post in Capodochino Corapo. His name is Marriott, and according to his reports he has been able to exercise some control over the field out there—"

The sick feeling in Morton was stronger. . . . Is it possible I've messed this thing up? He grew aware that the white face was saying gravely, "We haven't been able to contact Marriott this morning, Charles. Which is why I'm bringing you up to date. Will you rush out there and see what's happened?"

"Sir—" began Morton unsteadily.

He couldn't say more. He could only stand there and catch a faint, emotional glimpse of the disaster that threatened here.

"You may have wondered," Lauren't voice came as from a tunnel, so remote had everything become, "why I and a few of my top assistants have never left this part of the building. It's because this section has been protected against whatever is in that planetary energy field. We are connected to the Corapo defense."

Slowly Morton straightened. The world came partly back into focus. He echoed aloud, "This section is . . . protected?"

So that was the explanation for their immunity.

Hopeful again, he looked around the glittering room. Could it be that at this moment, while he was here, he also was protected? And that if he were to tell Laurent the truth, it would in this *protected* environment not instantly bring reaction?

Before he could decide, Laurent said, "What has especially disturbed us is that late last night this protective field, which Marriott had rigged for us, suddenly ceased to manifest. It's vital that you get over there and investigate."

As he finished speaking, he paused and squeezed his eyes hard.

He looked up after a long moment and said, "Excuse me.

All this seems to have affected me, and I am subject to periodic dizzy spells—I notice you have a similar affliction."

It was not a good moment. For that moment Morton couldn't speak.

Laurent continued, "I have one more point. As one of my amusements during an otherwise boring time of waiting, I have played the mental game of being Colonel Charles Morton." He smiled in that friendly way. "After reading one of your reports, I'd lie awake and imagine myself looking at the scenes you described. In fact, I would try to reconstruct your movements. As a strictly intellectual exercise, I have attempted to live your life as I imagined it."

He broke off. "Judging by the reports I have here on my desk, I was singularly unsuccessful in that effort." Ruefully he tapped the papers on his desk, said, "According to these accusations, you have been guilty of minor violations of the law these past few days: Escaping from a hospital, stealing an Irsk prisoner, and—"

Morton parted his lips.

He grew aware that the ambassador was holding up a hand, warningly. "No explanations now," Laurent smiled. "But I trust you will eventually be able to look your accusers in the eye and tell them that Intelligence officers must sometimes act quickly. On your way, colonel."

Morton did not move. Instead: "Do you trust Marriott?" he asked.

There was a long pause. The eyes in the white face widened a little: He's a human being," the older man said finally: "He's *got* to be on our side."

After a hesitation of his own, Morton nodded. "All right," he said simply, "where have I met you before?"

Silence. The gray eyes staring at him, widening a little. And then—

Laurent was on his feet. He came running around the gleaming, brilliant desk, his hand held out. "You've done it!" he said. "Congratulations, colonel!"

The next second he had grabbed Morton's hand and was shaking it vigorously. As he did so, he made certain statements about what Morton's question established about his personal development as a finite logic human being.

It was Morton who suddenly drew back. "Sir, are you saying that you yourself are nearly four hundred years old?"

"Yes." The white face was calm. "And the fact that you spotted me, which I suspected when you first came in, means that you can now be admitted to the first stage of the finite logic brotherhood. I'm delighted for you, colonel. It's the same story: thousands of hours of doing and thinking; and at last the cells begin to align."

"But," protested Morton faintly. "where *did* we meet before? And why don't I remember?"

Once again the reassuring smile. "We have never met, Charles. What happens is that eventually finite logic people know each other as such. Surely you've already had the female attraction."

He became abruptly somber. "However, let me caution you. We can be killed as easily as anyone. But if we survive violence, then our life span is considerable."

It was Morton's turn to brace himself. It seemed to him that the pure truth he had received deserved a minimum of candor in return. "Let me caution *you*, sir," he said. "Your action in trying to be me may have got you . . . connected . . . to my duplicate up in the magnetic field. How that will come out is not obvious to me at this time."

Having spoken, he spun around and left the room.

Twenty-Six

HE DROVE with Luftelet to Capodochino Corapo. There was heavy traffic all the way. Observing that scene again, seeing the vaguely smiling drivers as they careened toward them just across the double line, Morton thought: It can't be that these crazy little cars will still be driving here a thousand years from now.

But of course finite logic said they would. And also that equally mad people (though in a somewhat improved society) would be driving them. The intermilieu motor had been standard for more than fourteen hundred years. Noisy it was, yes; but it operated on the "dead" part of the atmosphere, the nitrogen, and so its fuel was forever free. Hard to imagine an improvement on that. . . . Perhaps some genius would find a way to silence the little blasters.

After a little, Morton made a small attempt to placate Luftelet. He said, "Aristotle's syllogisms were a joke long before the twentieth century. Yet they have a certain purity. When applied to a proper subject in their frame, they proved true enough."

There was no reply. The older man was at the wheel, and he was peering grimly forth. It did seem to Morton that Luftelet's expression changed to contempt.

Morton persisted, "Most of the things that a syllogism could prove everybody knew. What it couldn't prove everybody knew, too. So in ancient days learned men, having nothing else, used the method where it applied. Life was kind of simple. Grim but simple. And so the human brain bridged the gap between the system and the reality. The "modern" logic that succeeded the syllogistic system in the twentieth century was bravely named. Sort of like here, finally, is the truth. . . . It wasn't."

It was an either-or idea. "Where Edward is, Mary isn't. Most useful in the great switching systems of computers and such, they said. Those were the days when if a switch or a transistor or a relay didn't work, the engineer would say irritably, "For God's sake, get us another R2B unit."

At some deep level of his being, he believed (with "modern" logic) that all R2B units belonged to a "set," and they *should* work, damn it.

And that system kept things in operation, because the human brain sort of understood that sometimes Mary did try to occupy the same space as Edward. And the gap between the set theory and the certainties of the Venn diagrams on the one hand and, on the other, the reality that as the machines grew more complicated, engineers learned from sad experience to furnish backup equipment that could take over in the event of a failure. People even worked out sophisticated MTBF (Mean Time Before Failure) theories for innumerable components.

But there was a day in the twenty-first century when (so the news reports later stated) every machine everywhere stopped. Obviously that was never literally true. But that was the way it looked.

For a day or more science confronted the nightmare product of a logic system that was based upon a mathematics which stated that there is such a thing as a dozen eggs or a dozen duplicate transistors—in short, a "set" of eggs or of anything.

Not true.

On that day of total (?) stoppage, every egg on Earth stood up and said, in effect, "I too am an individual."

Of course, the things that really made this point were the components of a computerized America and West Europe. No logic system would ever be able to deal with so much individuality. And so the finite logic on which modern (39th century) computers worked consisted of—

Morton's mentalizing ended abruptly. He was snatched out of the world of thought and precipitated back into the universe of New Naples. A visual feast greeted his eyes.

Their little monstrosity had roared around another green hill. This time, instead of more closely packed houses, the land fell away suddenly. The city almost disappeared from view. To the left was the ocean shoreline. Beyond, shafts and flashes of soft light sparkled from an opalescent sea. For several, breathless moments, as he gazed out over the remoter crystalline waters, Morton had one of the rare views of shining Capri (usually buried in mist).

It reminded him . . . what Marriott had said about finally finding the place where you wanted to spend your life. Marriott, of course, had made the decision quite a while ago. But it was a thought which had never really impinged on Charles Morton.

Suddenly it tempted him. Why not? he asked himself. Why not marry that girl? After all, he was no angel. He had been making love to females for a long, long time, indeed, at least until he was suddenly offended by his methods.

Spending one's life in beautiful New Naples might be— what? Once more a train of thought came to an end. He blinked. . . . Am I out of my mind? he wondered, appalled. The whole planet was a boiling inferno, for God's sake.

He leaned back, breathing hard. And guessed that there were other false Mortons in the circuit now and their collective feeling had nearly conned him. As he realized that, the beautiful sea disappeared. They curved around a height, past some green and rounded hills, and then down a steep slope that led straight into the outskirts of Capodochino Corapo.

At Morton's direction, Luftelet drove as close to the military post as other parked cars permitted. The two men climbed out. Luftelet walked down the street to the door of the building. Morton headed across the road. He turned and gazed at the strange little structure.

It seemed to crouch close to the ground. It was flat and dark in shape and color. Architecturally, the mountains behind it demanded shingled peaks and towering spires. It had none. The roof was black brown metal. The walls were a dull, corrugated substance without windows.

There *was* considerable size. A spreadoutness suggested many rooms inside. A barracks might conceivably look like that. Big or small, Morton knew, didn't matter. Size was not

124

a factor where a cubic inch can hold thousands of resistors, coils, transistors and other electronic components. The outer and inner "skins" of this particular military post consisted of a chemical substance that was superresistant to impacts, energies, and, in fact, *all* negating forces. Between the two skins of that immensely hard substance was such an array of receptors, scanners and receivers that no human brain could even grasp the complexity. More than a hundred constructing computers had reasoned it together.

Disconcerting to discover at this late date that a James Marriott had been put in charge of it; a man with an impressive Ph.D. in physics but with no emotional equivalent of a degree in loyalty—

It was a minute later. He had walked to the door. There was a little time, then, while he established his total take-over credentials—and discovered that Marriott had departed in the wee hours that morning and had not returned.

"He had us call an ambulance, sir; and he took his patient with him."

"Patient?" echoed Morton.

"Yes, sir, the unconscious body of a woman."

"Do you know the woman's name?"

"I have it here—" The guard bent over his book and read out. "She came in two nights ago; Isolina Ferraris."

So this is where she came; I'll be damned, thought Morton. He was unable to dredge up any other thought about it.

Somewhat blanked out by the information, he led the way into the building. It turned out—Luftelet reported—that only the power had been shut off which connected with the protective field of the Negotiating Palace. . . . A deliberate act? Morton wondered. And, obviously, that was the first deduction one could make about such an action.

It seemed minor; almost a pettish thing for Marriott to have done. Yet it had some of the aspect of a man burning his bridges. Morton stood by as Luftelet closed four relays.

"Is the palace protected again?" Morton wanted to know.

In replying Luftelet made a series of obscure technical remarks. It required all of Morton's ability for careful listening to evaluate the words as meaning yes. Standing there, he suppressed the impulse to have another try at breaking down this madman's barriers to communication. Finally, he walked, instead, off long the gleaming corridor to the instrument room. One look; and his fleeting impulse to check the equipment personally collapsed. The long, narrow chamber ran all the way around the outer walls of the building, and it

125

was absolutely jammed, with just enough room for some equivalent of a catwalk.

In this world, Morton thought grayly, we really have to depend on trustworthy technical help. . . . He met Luftelet a few minutes later in Marriott's private office.

. . . No alternative, it seemed to a reluctant Morton. For all he knew, this was the twelfth hour minus a few minutes on Diamondia. Perhaps, with Luftelet, the old, old ploy of responsibility would achieve what direct reason could not.

Aloud he said, "Major Luftelet, you will remain here in charge of this post until further notice. You outrank Captain Marriott—in case he returns. . . ."

"*Yes, sir!* I'll have my effects sent over."

"Before I leave," said Morton, "is there anything else that you should tell me?"

In checking out the building controls, Luftelet had observed several automatic aspects. But he considered these to be too "technical" to be brought to Morton's attention. So he said, "No, sir."

After making his denial, the major stood calm and straight. His eyes were clear and untroubled. His mouth was innocent. And his whole manner radiated the purity of what an honest fellow this was: supremely intelligent yet carrying himself with the quiet, courteous restraint of one who knew the limitations of untrained people.

"Good," said Morton.

He led the way to the outer door. He actually stepped outside before turning once more to look at Luftelet, who had paused beside the guard station inside. At this final moment, it seemed to the superior officer that he must do his level best to think of questions that would alert the other man to the necessity for good communication.

"In the event," Morton said, "that I trigger this whole machine into action, will it all work?"

"It's ready for operation, sir," was the reply.

"It will," asked Morton, "actually work as a unit and do what it is constructed to do? In other words, according to your figure of 138,000, this building can keep itself in repair for about nine minutes when it is fighting?"

"That is correct, sir," said Major Luftelet.

Something in the man's manner continued to bother Morton. "Tell me again what it does when it's at peak operation," he said.

Luftelet told him patiently. It was exactly as Morton had

126

previously understood. And yet—again the tone of the telling, the attitude of it, disturbed him. He made a final effort.

"Major," he said frankly, "it is very likely that at a key moment I shall, in fact, instruct this marvelous machine into its fighting posture. If at that time it does not operate correctly, we may lose this planet; and at very least you will be court-martialed if it does not do exactly as it is supposed to. Bearing that in mind, is there *anything* that you would like to add to your reassurance? This is probably the last time I'll have a chance to discuss it with you."

If the earnestness of his voice impressed the heavy-set man, it did not show. Luftelet said with dignity, "If I am ever court-martialed, sir, and I have the opportunity to call on my peers to verify the technical expertness of my check out, I shall be completely exonerated. Is that what you want to know?"

It was—in a way. Morton turned, intending to walk to his car. Then once more, stopped. Poised there, conscious of the scores of things he must still do today, he nevertheless took time to consider what he had gained from this visit. Morton tried to tell himself that what the other man meant and what he desired to be were in fact the same thing.

Had he, through Luftelet, converted this building into a weapon that he could count on to help him in the coming storm?

Reluctantly he decided that he had not.

It was a down moment. What bothered him, he realized, was that he had apparently accomplished neither of his purposes in coming to the post. His second intent, to have it out with Marriott, was naturally nullified by Marriott's total absence from the scene.

If only, he thought, I could control my interaction with the Morton duplicate in the field up there. . . . As he had that thought, his awareness embraced the possibility that had occurred to him on his way back from Nucea. *Be* the duplicate. Sort of let yourself do an internal shift. Like a visual illusion. It even seemed to him that he could test the concept by attempting to locate Lieutenant Bray. And then, and only then, after he felt secure in the process, go after Marriott.

It was a moment of unwariness.

A baritone voice said inside his head, "This is the Lositeen Weapon speaking to you through the Mahala System. The Mahala and I have arrived at an agreement; and we'd like to know exactly where you are right now."

"Hey!" said a startled Morton.

Major Luftelet, being slightly slow-witted, stared at the crumpled body where it lay partly against the door jamp. As he stood there blinking in astonishment (mixed with a feeling of justice done and done quickly), he heard the door guard call out the lieutenant on duty.

About a minute after that, Morton had been brought into the post hallway. And the guard was on the phone again. This time he called an ambulance.

Naturally, Luftelet meticulously did his duty. He waited until the Irsk ambulance attendants loaded the limp body into their machine.

And he watched the air ambulance fly off.

Twenty-Seven

. . . Morton seemed to be lying on his back. And the body he was in must have been asleep, for it stirred and awakened.

The thoughts of David Kirk came into his mind..

"Now, *that*," said the baritone voice, "is what gives us hope for the future. You aimed for Lieutenant Lester Bray, but you mind-brothered with Special Assistant David Kirk. The Mahala System and I believe that if that ability can be developed to include other members of the human race, we can extend Mahala power over the whole of Man's galaxy—"

Blankness. Some astonishment. . . . Afterward, Morton realized that his subsequent actions were relatively rational. First he correctly deduced that his precise analysis of how he might shift from his body to his duplicate had started him into this predicament. And, far more significant, his connecting up with David Kirk was proof that his efforts to confuse the darkness had succeeded.

All those male and female Diamondians and Earth federation soldiers—ten thousand of them, for heaven's sake—were now members of a Colonel Charles Morton "set." Kind of chilling that the darkness also thought that was a good thing. But that was its delusion, and evidently also its long-run goal with all life in the universe. The Irsk had clearly been well equalized when the Diamondian colonists arrived. Every Irsk was the same (to the darkness) as every other Irsk, though they had retained a modicum of individuality through their long, strange, dissimilar names. So, in effect, they had survived by being different in that one thing.

But such a condition didn't apply to what he had done. All his people had the same name. . . . I'm hidden. In this situation that's what counts. Now it-they can't find *me*.

Morton was exhilarated yet thoughtful. Did he have anything to say to David Kirk? He could think of nothing.

He deduced that the big test for him was could he shift anywhere? To anyone? As he had that consideration, he felt shaken by a sudden fear of failure. And then—

With total determination, he did the mental illusion of visualizing himself "up" in the field.

Instantly, he was there in a gray mist. . . . It *worked*.

The victory was so tremendous that for long moments he did and thought nothing at all. Finally, consciously, he relaxed. And for the first time looked at the implications of the darkness and the Lositeen Weapon being together. He said in a tentative, questioning tone, "How did you two join up?"

His question was ignored. Instead—"Where is your body?" repeated the baritone voice.

A pause. A silence. . . . It really wouldn't hurt to tell, Morton thought. Because I'm at the one place, the Corapo building, where the darkness cannot get at me.

What held him secretive was another awareness: His professional policy was never to volunteer information to a potential enemy. The same concept extended to this situation required that he take no immediate action of any kind.

. . . His feeling: The slightest error in judgement would be fatal. Remember, he told himself, this is the being that proposed *total* extermination of the Diamondian people.

A timeless consideration now took over and held him where he was. . . . Have to think through every move and do nothing and be nowhere. And wait.

Had to believe that the mass murder threat talk *could* be real. So stay where you are until—

He had no idea.

Twenty-Eight

Isolina woke up in a plane and experienced the proprioceptive sensation of flying. There were two Irsk sitting side by side up front, one of them as pilot. In the seat beside her own (which had been lowered into bed position) sat a gloomy looking Marriott.

In observing these things she must have moved. For Marriott turned in his seat and gazed down at her. "You're awake," he said unnecessarily.

Isolina's mind had already leaped to the truth. "That drink," she accused, "It knocked me out."

Marriott nodded unhappily. "I didn't believe talking would do any good," he said.

By this time the woman was experiencing warning signals in her body. An unusual lassitude. Weakness. A strong need to go to the bathroom.

"How long have I been out?" she demanded.

"This is the second day." He spoke reluctantly. "I didn't know what to do with you."

It took time to absorb that information, to feel the shock of the hours that had elapsed. Yet she was thinking again. Her next words reached past many intermediate mysteries. She said simply. "What do you know about the darkness?"

This time his hesitation was momentary only. Then, in a voice that trembled slightly, he described how he had been defeated by Morton.

Isolina was incredulous. "You mean Colonel Morton is now and has been for two days at the control center of the darkness?"

Marriott confessed, "I overreached myself in opening the door of Lieutenant Bray's car. But the fact is, I wanted Morton off the planet . . . the sharp way he questioned me when he came to see me right after his arrival. I decided he was a dangerous man for my purposes."

The woman beside him was visibly thinking about what he had told her. Her expression grew troubled. Then abruptly— a thought:

"B-but—" Isolina protested, "Colonel Morton must already

have been in control when I saw him. It didn't seem to do him any good."

"I'm sure," said Marriott, "he hasn't the faintest idea what to do, and I'm not planning to tell him. But I lost everything."

"What did you lose? What is the darkness?"

Marriott countered, "What's a government?"

"An apparatus for governing."

"No." He smiled wanly, "A government is your agreement to be governed."

"But that's ridiculous. That means there's nothing there, really."

"True."

"That's the darkness?"

"That's it."

"Nothing?"

"Well—" said Marriott, "a government is as strong as the agreement it has managed to elicit from its populace. In the case of the Irsk, with a billion energy duplicates of their bodies as part of the magnetic field of this planet, that is slightly colossal."

"Then what's the trouble?"

"The Diamondians."

"How do you mean?"

As Marriott earnestly described it for her, the Diamondian emotional character had gradually produced a reaction in the essentially receptive Irsk. The resultant volatile emotional energy had of course been duplicated "up there in the field" also.

"Then apparatus itself is disturbed. It's as if the army and the civil service have got out of hand, and everybody is beginning to do as he pleases. If you can picture all the Diamondians on this planet completely out of control—"

"But that's the way the men *are*," Isolina protested.

Marriott's face broke into a wan smile. "No, no, my dear. That's only the way it occasionally seems to a perceptive woman. But the fact is, Diamondian males do behave."

"But so do Irsk—even more."

"The duplicates are discharging too much energy into the field." Flatly, "I'm telling you."

The woman's mind had taken another jump forward. "What will now happen?" she asked.

Before Marriott could answer, the plane they were in went into a steep dive. "What's the matter?" Marriott called forward.

"We've got to land at this edge of the Gyuma Ravine," one of the Irsk replied. "The woman will have to be tied and carried on a stretcher."

Marriott said sharply, "Who gave an order like that?"

"Mgdabltt. He and his forces have taken over the ship."

"Oh!"

Marriott sank back, an unhappy scowl on his face. The woman stared at him questioningly. The physicist finally managed a tense smile. "I'm the deposed king," he said, "and suddenly I have to walk just like anyone else."

There was a brief silence between the two human beings. Isolina sat up carefully and adjusted her seat to an upright position. Her face had an uneasy expression on it. "The Gyuma Ravine?" she said. "That's the most dangerous spot on the whole front right now. What are we doing here?"

"The ship is here." He managed a wan smile. "When I first took over the Mahala system—"

"The what?"

"For heaven's sake, you don't think it's really called the darkness, just because the human brain blacks out a little during the five minute pulse peak. Anyway," he continued, "some years ago the Irsk captured one of the large Diamondian spaceships. I had it buried under a cliff in the ravine. It was sort of my headquarters, like the palace of the king—"

Isolina's thought had been leaping ahead of his words, testing the many possibilities of what he was describing. Abruptly, she interrupted him. "So that's why you had the peace missions come to the ravine."

"Who would have imagined," he groaned, "that they'd start a major war, so that now my remote haven is where the Irsk-Diamondian war is at its worst. I didn't plan it that way, I assure you."

"B-but—" said Isolina.

Her voice faltered. Through the transparencies of the ship, where until now only sky had been visible, was suddenly a hillside, a forest meadow, a glint of a stream.

A tiny thump as they landed. From the edge of the clearing a dozen Irsk started toward the small aircraft.

Fear came; hopelessness. "James," she said distractedly, "why did you bring me into such a deadly situation?"

"You're the general's daughter," he said. "These people are like Diamondians. They can see some kind of a vague possibility in that. So they insisted."

Pause. Realization. Then anxiously, "Before you let them tie me, be sure I have a chance to go to the bathroom."

"You'll have to do it on the ground," said Marriott.

"Of course. Anywhere. But quick!"

Twenty-Nine

THE GREAT, HOT, BLUE Diamondian sun had come up that morning on a planet leaning, in a manner of speaking, over the cliff of disaster. Its instant burning rays seethed down on New Naples, so that people emerging into the open from their air-conditioned homes shuddered with anticipation of a boiling morning, a steaming afternoon and a cooked evening.

Duplicates of those rays poked down through the foliage of the Gyuma Ravine jungle to where, in the half gloom below, a group of Diamondians trudged along a forest pathway. Two of the group of about thirty persons carried a stretcher on which was the unconscious body of David Kirk, whom everyone believed was Colonel Charles Morton of the Negotiating Committee.

The members of the Diamondian peace mission had their instructions from their Irsk guides: to proceed forward to a certain clearing. There wait until late afternoon. At a signal, the delegates would go forward into a ship. Inside would be the Irsk peace mission. The meeting would take place there.

No one was to be armed. On that there were no qualifications; not even a knife, nothing.

"We do not," the Irsk message had stated, "want a repetition of the error which nullified the previously planned meeting."

The Diamondian leaders had promised faithfully.

. . . As David Kirk stirred on the stretcher, he had a memory of a smug remark he had once made about himself. The remark had been that the awakening of a David Kirk must never be confused with an ordinary male emerging from sleep. David was a young man approximately twenty-eight years of age. For nearly a decade (after he worked out a personal solution in relation to the women's unions—money) he had come to each morning beside a good-looking prostitute or other available female.

No exaggeration (he had pointed out suavely) that David Kirk, both waking and sleeping, was in an amoral state. So much so that during the drowsy instants between sleep and wakefulness when presumably a kind of childlike purity dominated even hardened criminals . . . there was nothing like that in David.

His awakening, triggered when Morton accidentally mind-brothered with him, did produce a moment of shocked surprise. Just for an instant, as his eyes flickered open, he saw the jungle. For an equally startled few seconds, he realized that he was tied hand and foot. . . . Then the deviousness took over.

So he did *not* have an impulse to speak and identify himself. Instead, he lay with closed eyes and cautiously considered his strange condition.

That was the one thing he failed to get away with. A Diamondian cannot be fooled on small things. The momentary opening of Kirk's eyes had been noticed by everyone near the stretcher. There was a smug exchange of knowing looks among those who had observed the eye movements.

Quickly the information was passed along the procession to the leaders. They, all of them, came back to see for themselves. They also nodded knowingly as they observed, with a Diamondian's perception, the false sleep state of the man they believed was Colonel Morton.

After brief consultation the procession came to a halt there in the jungle. The stretcher was put down on the ground. While the Irsk guides waited politely off to one side, the head of the delegation, his two immediate aides, two of the four legal experts, the military liaison officer (a Diamondian colonel) and his assistant (a captain) converged around the prisoner-hostage.

After he had been poked a couple of times and twice spoken to: ("Colonel Morton, we know you are awake!"), David Kirk opened his eyes, accepted the false identity and requested permission to speak in private to his opposite number, the Diamondian colonel. The others reluctantly moved back. Kirk promptly informed the officer that his father was worth a hundred million federation dollars (which was true for David Kirk) and would unquestionably pay any ransom for his beloved son. He therefore called on the officer as a brother-in-arms to rescue him as soon as possible. He promised on his word as a colonel that the money would be paid privately. The round sum he mentioned was a million.

Naturally his Diamondian colleague made an immediate shrewd bargain that would also satisfy the other members of his own party. He offered Kirk-Morton his safety in exchange for the money and the reason the Irsk wanted control of the chief Intelligence officer of the Negotiating Committee. The reason—Kirk reached imaginatively but with a certain practical understanding, as he glibly spoke the explanation—was that because of his wealthy family, he, Morton, was the real ambassador negotiator. The Irsk had found this out. Recognizing that no deal would be permitted that was not satisfactory to Colonel Morton, they had conceived the scheme of forcing his consent to the new contract. And they had not realized that he would be glad to give his approval to *any* beneficent agreement.

This information, when transmitted to the other members of the peace delegation, seemed perfectly reasonable. His captors were relieved. A happy conviction swept down the line of men, the feeling that the success of their mission was now assured.

It was late afternoon when an Irsk scout appeared. He spoke briefly to the Irsk guides and then, after securing permission from the Diamondian leaders, walked over to David Kirk, bent down and asked him if he were indeed Colonel Charles Morton of the Negotiating Committee.

David, of course, said he was. When this information was transmitted by the Irsk mental communication via the darkness to the waiting Irsk delegation and by them to the group that was momentarily expecting Lositeen, who had the real Colonel Morton (Lieutenant Bray) with him, it created a puzzled state which no Irsk was emotionally qualified to deal with.

Yet, having learned their relation-to-human reactions from Diamondians, they took a definite pleasure in the fact that at least they would soon have both the real and the false Morton in their possession. That, they told themselves with satisfaction, would swiftly make it possible to settle the matter of identity.

Every Irsk also had an uneasy memory of a third Morton, who was being brought by air ambulance and was scheduled to land shortly. . . . Still, we'll have him, also, soon—

Thirty

NATURALLY GERHARDT hadn't quite known what had happened to him. The supertechnology of Intelligence gadgets that could hit out automatically when the heartbeat of the agent changed in a certain way, was within his frame of training. But he had never had such a device strike at him personally.

Lacking predefenses, he was overwhelmed.

Since the method used was not intended to be disabling or long lasting, he opened his eyes less than half an hour later.

And there he was in that situation. The plane. Zoolanyt. The two unconscious bodies.

With them his intent had been to achieve total control. So they would not awaken for another hour and would, of course, remain hypnotized for several days.

From the pilot's seat, Zoolanyt said, "I have your chemical gun, doctor, and I have the colonel's revolver. I am taking you all to the Gyuma Ravine." A casual tentacle pointed at Lositeen. "Getting him is the big event. But they're also interested in Colonel Charles Morton. There seem to be several Colonel Charles Mortons, and the leadership has received a communication from the darkness that the false ones must be exterminated, since they are causing a confusion."

It was more information than Gerhardt was qualified to digest immediately. Since he was not a man who admitted ignorance (if he could help it) he did not immediately ask for clarification.

He did toy with the idea of pretending to be scared but decided no.

Instead: "What about me?" he urged. "Why not just put me down somewhere?"

But Zoolanyt had his orders about that, also. "Your expert knowledge may be needed to deal with what your chemical weapon did to those two."

"You don't need me for that." He spoke halfheartedly. "They'll awaken spontaneously in an hour."

He didn't really expect that to change the decision that had already been made. And it didn't. Zoolanyt ignored the words.

The plane flew on. Gerhardt sat there, neither happy, afraid, angry nor sad. At twenty-six (he looked younger) he

136

had no personal feelings that he knew about: simply knowledge and trained responses.

Literally, his responses had been ground into his nervous system by artificial energies that matched the vital neural flows in his body and brain.

His response to a new situation like this was suspension of response.

So he waited; not blank, of course. It was his custom to review a patient's case history prior to the patient's arrival. There was no patient coming, but Bray and Lositeen were an analogous situation. Gerhardt reviewed every word and implication.

He decided for the interim: *I'll let them both think they're free.*

. . . After the two awakened, and later, after the craft landed, and there they were on the ground, Gerhardt maintained his no response status. Except, he found an opportunity in the jungle to whisper to Bray-Morton that false Mortons were going to be killed.

What to do finally?

No decision on that by Gerhardt. Judgement suspended. Response delayed.

Wait.

Thirty-One

THE FIRST TIME Morton mind-brothered, he aimed at Marriott.

A test. He said nothing. Just looked.

A jungle scene. . . . And, accidentally, apparently a key moment. A large group of Irsk guerrillas were coming across a clearing to where Marriott stood beside a stretcher, which was being held up by two Irsk. Marriott was gazing across the stretcher at the approaching group; and so Morton could only guess who was on the stretcher. The edge of it was barely visible from the corner of Marriott's eyes.

He guessed Isolina.

As the fighting dyl came up, the carriers lowered the stretcher to the grass. This action momentarily attracted Marriott's attention. He turned. Looked down. It was Isolina.

She looked forlorn. The beautiful Diamondian sometime prostitute was out here in the jungle where she could make no clever use of her body.

137

Was she afraid? There was a dullness in her brown eyes that reflected a lower energy state than fear—apathy, perhaps. Yet during those moments that Morton (through Marriott) stared at her, it was also obvious that she was not completely defeated. Something in her manner suggested that she was taking note of her surroundings; observing, listening.

Indeed, as he looked at her, she lifted herself and gazed at the new arrivals.

Marriott did the same. It was significant to Morton that the fighting dyl ignored their deposed leader and addressed the Irsk stretcher-bearers. "Is this," one of the newcomers asked, "the girl friend of the one who has the mind-brother?"

"Yes."

The guerrilla glided forward in the tentacled fashion and stood above the woman. "In your opinion," he addressed her, "what is your boyfriend, the Negotiating Colonel trying to achieve?"

Marriott had turned again, and so Morton not only heard but saw the interchange. It was clear from the expression on Isolina's face that being directly spoken to had alerted her. She was visibly thinking hard, as she said after a moment's hesitation, "Colonel Morton is involved in many negotiating activities. To which one do you refer?"

"A confusion has arisen as to which is Colonel Morton's real body. Normally this would be a desirable condition—interchangeability makes it easier for the darkness to deal with large groups of people. However, in this situation we need to find some way of identifying the real one correctly. Is there any clue that you can give us?"

The look on Isolina's face showed that it was a difficult question for her. But she clearly had no intention of making such an admission, for she said quickly, "As everyone knows, the Negotiating Committee is here to achieve an Irsk victory, and unless the Irsk do something to turn the Committee members against them, the Colonel Morton who is in favor of the Irsk winning this war, will be the real one."

It was—Morton had to admit it—an impressively skillful dialogue on the part of Isolina Ferraris. Highly disturbing, therefore, to realize that he could still think of no way to save her life.

. . . Morton did his second mind-brothering with the quartet of Bray, Gerhardt, Lositeen and Zoolanyt, utilizing Dr. Gerhardt as his viewpoint.

Impression of neutralness. The scene: trees, brush, a narrow tail; everything hemmed in. The young psychiatrist

138

walked directly behind Lositeen and though they were only a few yards from each other, he kept losing sight of that silent being, so dense was the jungle.

Morton could hear sounds from behind Gerhardt. Presumably, the noises were caused by Bray and Zoolanyt, but not once during this initial contact did Gerhardt turn his head.

The very coldness of the man was ultimately admirable. Literally, Gerhardt was not disturbed by his situation.

. . . On his second contact with the little group, Morton mind-brothered with Lositeen. And that was sad. A blank mind watched the jungle trail and seemed to draw its responses automatically from a subawareness level. Morton in his training period had been chemical; and he had never had a total shut off like this.

It was sad that the Irsk, who had seemed so mighty a factor because of his present life guardianship if the Lositeen Weapon, was suddenly a nothing. Yet it looked that way. The kindly disposed, hard working antirebel presented a conditioned appearance that was as close to zero as a living creature could be.

Could I dehypnotize him? Morton wondered.

Since he was still taking no actions, still only looking, still with no plan for coping with the vast power of the enemy . . . he merely thought that and did nothing.

Soon there would have to be action against the colossus in the sky. But not yet.

Back up in the field, Morton told himself: It has to be a victory that I can now do mind-brothering on my own decision. . . . From this vantage point, with his body either in a bed in the Corapo military post (preferably) or in a nearby hospital, he could for the first time contact *anyone*—except, apparently, the people who were in the Colonel Charles Morton lineup.

He had tried twice more for Bray; and once (in those two attempts) found himself sharing the brain of a Diamondian, who walked along a street of a Diamondian city that Morton did not recall having seen before. For a few minutes, he observed a Diamondian male's inner world; then, shuddering, he withdrew. The second attempt, he mind-brothered with an Earth federation soldier who was making love to a prostitute.

Interesting but discouraging. He very much wanted a conversation with Bray. But, apparently, that was a 10,000 to one chance and therefore not practicable.

Where else could he go that would be valuable to him now? What people should he contact? He made several attempts to visualize the Irsk duplicate in the Gyuma jungle, the luminous creature that had talked to Joaquin after the decimation of the Diamondian peace group.

Got nothing. Which was slightly baffling. But it again emphasized that the enemy was not really down on the planet. Because, aside from that one try (and it was a failure), he really could not think of anyone else (besides Marriott) to mind-brother with.

Should I talk to Marriott? . . . Once more, he decided *. . . not yet.*

The next time he contacted Gerhardt, it was shortly before dusk and another key moment.

The route of the little group of four had finally brought them to the top of a hill. And there, below and around, was the view of the Gyuma Ravine that Morton had been hoping for.

Everybody stopped. Gerhardt did so to catch his breath after the climb. Through the psychiatrist's glasses Morton saw a jungle land, already darkened by the long shadows from a sun that was sinking toward the west. The trees spread like a mist of gray and black, and some green to a remoter distance than his preconception of it.

Shadows, thick growth, faraway cliff walls—it was impressively sizable. Sometimes (he thought) one tended to be overwhelmed by interstellar, multi-light-year separations and failed to realize that sixteen miles of jungle three miles wide constituted a respectable area, particularly for beings who were afoot.

The heights eye look greatly relieved him. The darkness, he thought, will have a hard time pinpointing anyone in this huge, he relished the meaning, wilderness.

He accompanied the two humans and two aliens down the far side of the steep hill. And was still with them on a stretch of open ground, still up above the floor of the ravine, when there was a sound and a flash of light ahead. Lositeen, who had remained in front of Gerhardt, stopped. The friendly Irsk reached back with one tentacle, which he placed on Gerhardt's arm urging him down.

As Gerhardt sank into some long grass, Bray crawled up beside him. A moment later, Zoolanyt came up from Bray's rear, and he also knelt down. During the minute of silence that ensued, Morton attempted to reconstruct the sound that Gerhardt had heard.

To his practiced awareness it was an energy noise; the kind

140

that metal can make when a flow of electrons or protons or other particles is set in motion by overriding force.

But there are friendly energy sounds and unfriendly. This noise had in it, as Morton now relayed it through his awareness, something of the unpleasant, sinister quality of a steel rattlesnake.

Power!

It occurred to him that the flash of brightness was a light counterpart of the sound. In his analogy he conceived it to be the rattler striking with a flickering movement of its steel bright head.

. . . Disconcerting, after reacting to the event out there with such an eerie stream of speculation, to realize what they had witnessed was probably an intense electrical manifestation, deadly, not to be dismissed as minor, definitely an enormous output—but mundane.

He waited there, aware that, incredibly, the psychiatrist remained in the same frozen, no response state as earlier. It was Bray who broke the verbal silence of the group. "What," he asked, breathless, "was *that!*"

The two Irsk didn't know. Zoolanyt said presently, "I've just talked to Mgdabltt. And he has no idea either. He is anxious to question Colonel Charles Morton."

The real Colonel Charles Morton, hearing those words through Gerhardt's ears, decided that it was time to act. Night was falling. His observational stance had provided him with a priceless opportunity to think and to look and to experience the fantastic ability to mind-brother.

With that behind him, what should he do first? Talk to Marriott, obviously.

Like a wraith, he faded out of Gerhardt's mind. In point of distance, he went about three miles. In terms of reality, light-years.

Thirty-Two

STRAIGHTFORWARDNESS.

Morton's duplicate somewhere inside Marriott's brain said aloud, "Captain, I have just this minute mind-brothered with you. I'd like to talk to you."

There was a long pause after he spoke the greeting. During

the pause, Morton was able to observe that the group of guerrillas and the two Irsk who carried the stretcher with Isolina on it, and Marriott, were walking along at the bottom of a cliff. Marriott, as it quickly developed, brought up the rear.

The physicist was quick. He slowed. He fell back several steps then said in a low voice, "What do you want?"

"Is there any way," Morton asked, "that we can work together and defeat the——" he hesitated over the word but only for a few seconds, "Mahala System? You saw the fireworks just now, didn't you?"

Immediate astonishing reaction. Marriott's lips quivered. Tears came into his eyes. Startling to feel another man's emotions so directly. But Morton felt them, and they were disconcertingly intense.

"We're all in extreme danger," Marriott whispered. "What we saw is only a tiny sample. Diamondia is about to become a shambles. The Earth federation forces will be exterminated. The Diamondian people are on the verge of being killed to the last man, woman and child. And even the Irsk may not survive. I can't at this moment explain why it's holding back at all, but I know that the only hope we have is if I can get back the control I lost to you."

To Morton it sounded like an attempt to overwhelm him. But unfortunately it also felt like truth. He addressed Marriott again. "Why don't we have a discussion? The other night I said I was open to helping you. Maybe we can bypass that election and just give control back to you. Can we? I'm willing. Will the Irsk permit it?"

Marriott laughed, a sharp, barking laugh of disdain. Amazing the instant change of emotion in the man, from deep terror to cynicism.

Marriott said arrogantly, "They never had any say in my original control. And if you mean it—and if we can work out a method of return whereby you don't learn what my control system was—then they'll have no say now."

As he heard those words and that tone, Morton had a thought about Marriott, not for the first time: *This is not an easy man to like. . . .* But obviously that mustn't be a factor. In a crisis, mere personality madness was immaterial. He had in his time found many able men hard to take. But every one of them had at the decisive moment been on the side of the human race.

So there was no second choice, really. Marriott it had to be. "Consider it settled," Morton said hurriedly. "But tell me,

142

since you're so dangerous to it, why didn't the darkness destroy you after you were deposed?"

"You don't understand," was the reply. "It's logical within its frame. I'm not dangerous to it *now*. Besides, I'm always connected to the Corapo defense, so I don't believe it has ever thought of attacking me. Then, too, it has a hard time killing anyone by selection. It deals in large groups, not individuals. It probably knows where all the cities are, and it will first wreck all buildings with iron and steel in them—which is just about every house and structure on the planet. Then it will continuously stir up rock that has iron in it. . . . If you can, picture walking along an open countryside and suddenly the ground under you, with you on it, is jerked up a hundred feet. That's what we saw. There was an enormous electrical discharge when that happened."

His voice, as he spoke, was hoarse. He seemed to have forgotten his companions a short distance ahead. It was too loud. He was overheard. The nearest Irsk slowed and turned. The large, misty blue eyes stared at Marriott. Then: "Oh, somebody's mind-brothering with you." The guerrilla was tolerant. "Can't you just whisper your replies like the rest of us do?"

The dyl turned without waiting for an answer and glided on.

Marriott said in a low voice, "We're very close to the ship. Where's your body?" When Morton hesitated, the physicist urged, "I've got to know where you are for what I'm going to do."

Morton temporized, "Suppose I tell you when you're ready."

The other man agreed at once. "But that means you've got to stay with me, so that I can communicate with you at a moment's notice."

The requirement startled Morton. Because it had the black and white characteristic of a puzzle. He thought: Really, everywhere I look the puzzle aspect continues. . . .

Truth was, he could think of no other place where he ought to be or go. He *did* want to talk briefly to Isolina as soon as he could figure out a way to help her. But that was all.

On that basis, with that one reservation, he agreed.

And missed a momentous meeting.

Thirty-Three

IT WAS HALF AN HOUR LATER. Dusk misted everything. Lositeen, who was still in front, stopped. He glanced back at Gerhardt and actually seemed to be himself for that moment. He said in his gentle voice, "There's somebody coming. A duplicate of something. Not an Irsk."

Bray and Zoolanyt came up to where Gerhardt and Lositeen waited. The four stared along the dim trail at the . . . demon.

There was still light farther, higher, up. And so the luminous being was correspondingly hard to see. His head, though not manlike or Irsk-like, was egg shaped—In those first moments, Bray had a strong impression of a leonine being. His eyes were wide apart, round and golden in color.

He paused less than fifteen feet from the little group, and he said in a voice that had an odd lisp to it, "Colonel Charles Morton, I wish to speak to you. Come closer."

No holding back on such a direct request. Bray shuffled forward reluctantly.

Night was falling rapidly, and in the long spans of half-light that was dusk in the jungle it was progressively harder to see. Under his breath Bray uttered critical comments on the bad luck that had brought about this meeting at such an unfortunate time. But better now (he realized) than five minutes hence.

What he could see was a figure at least a head taller than himself. It had none of the substance of a solid body. It stood waiting for him in front of a large, fronded plant—and he could see the plant through it.

Bray came to within four feet of it and couldn't force his legs to move another step. This is a brand new situation, he thought. There are no precedents. He remembered Professor Pocatelli's statement: ". . . *they can kill.*"

It did not kill. It talked. It said, in that lisping voice, "I am a duplicate of one of the creators of the Mahala System. My original self departed more than two thousand Diamondian years ago. But I, the duplicate, remained in this area of space to act as monitor and guide.

"It is my duty to ensure that the Mahala System takes over

this part of the galaxy. Those who oppose must die. Those who accept become part of the system. Our ultimate goal is to include all life, galactic and intergalactic, in the Mahala communication network. When ten years ago Captain James Marriott took over from me, he did so by a method that did not affect the alarm system in distant Mahala centers."

"What was that method?" Bray asked boldly.

"Through me he ruled—"

Brief blankness of mind; a striving to grasp. Then: For heaven's sake, he thought, that would be like some royal aide or prime minister of long ago Earth getting control of the king and acting in his name.

He saw with instant insight why it had been impossible under such circumstances for Morton to have moved directly into the control center of the darkness. The only way to it was via this being.

Momentarily, what Marriott had done impressed Bray. What a masterful way of manipulating a vast system.

The feeling *was* momentary. Something about Marriott bothered Bray. *He did it for himself*—that was the uneasy analysis.

The creature who stood on that shadowy trail was silent as Bray had his own private thoughts. Bray said hastily, "What do we do next?"

"Free me!"

"You mean free you from Marriott's control?"

"Yes."

"What will you do when you're free?"

"Who would have thought," said the being, and its tone was suddenly emotional in a critical way, "that such a life form as the Diamondians could ever possibly exist. At the beginning, of course, I simply ignored them. But when the disturbance began ten years ago, that was no longer possible. So the Diamondians must be eliminated."

"You mean *exterminated*?"

"Yes."

The young officer consciously braced himself and then said what had to be spoken: "What you ask will never be tolerated by men anywhere. It is also not to Man's advantage to have somebody else take over this part of the galaxy and align or kill all the people in it. The Mahala"—he fumbled the word but said it anyway—"policy to destroy anyone who resists is a form of cruelty that will never be acceptable. Make that clear to your superiors."

During the pause that followed, Bray thought, awed: *I*

have just declared war on behalf of the human race. . . .
Well, so be it.

He had a second thought: Is that what it told Joaquin?
. . . Boy, what a total loss that turned out to be.

As he stood there, the misty creature turned away from
him and walked off along the trail. In a few seconds it was
out of sight.

As Bray rejoined his companions, he realized he was trembling in spite of himself. It had not been, in truth, a really
satisfactory interview.

Because, ridiculously, he had had a kind of a hope about
this being.

Which was now ended.

Thirty-Four

ABOUT TWENTY MINUTES went by. The four emerged suddenly onto what seemed to be a large open area beside a stream.

Shadowy figures moved toward them. Zoolanyt said hastily,
"Do not resist. We have arrived, and I have told them who
you are."

Seen close by, the newcomers became recognizable as Irsk.
As they came up, their tentacles grabbed Bray and Gerhardt
roughly. Bray stood acquiescent while his hands and ankles
were bound, and he was aware of Gerhardt being similarly
treated. There was no pause. The moment he was tied, he
was given a hard shove. He started to fall, but before he hit
the ground tentacles caught him and lifted him onto a
stretcher. At which, almost without pause, there was forward
motion.

The night around him was as black as pitch. But Bray grew
aware presently that he was being carried into an enclosed
space. Was it a ship, as he had been told it would be? His
eyes detected vague metallic gleams. So it must be.

A long corridor (so it was a big vessel) and then the sound
of a door clanging open. Light flooded. . . . As he was eased
in, he had impressions of a large room. To his left, behind a
long table, were more than a score of Diamondians. Some
stood. Some sat.

His was a fleeting look. He saw bright eyes and red, sweaty
faces. At that point he grew aware that he was being taken to

146

where several dozen Irsk stood against a back wall with several open doors behind them.

During the several moments it required for him to be carried to his destination, Bray had time to flick his gaze over the rest of the large room. A man stood off to one side; and he was conspicuous because he did not look like a Diamondian and wore a uniform. Bray recognized Captain James Marriott. The thin-faced man seemed very pale under the brilliant lights. Bray sent a quick glance at the stretcher beside which Marriott stood, but he could not make out who was in it; a woman, it seemed like.

There was a second stretcher somewhat nearer the Diamondians. A man occupied it. His face, as he glanced at Bray, was sensationally familiar: David Kirk.

That was all Bray had time to observe.

At that moment his stretcher was tilted forward, and he was unceremoniously dumped from it. He landed on his bound feet in front of an Irsk who wore the typical heavy clothing of these beings when they came to the "temperate" zones.

During all those initial seconds that Bray observed these fleeting details, he was fighting to retain his balance. His bound feet were almost too much for him; they held him while he leaned backward, forward, sideways, frontward in a series of jerky movements designed to shift his body's weight.

He made it. He stood there, breathing hard; and he realized for the first time that the whole place was absolutely stifling hot. Bray felt the sweat almost literally burst out of him. He was appalled. He breathed harder, striving to gasp in extra oxygen.

What bothered him most was the feeling that somehow he had to take charge of this whole situation. It cost him every bit of his willpower, but with a single stupendous effort he pushed the physical anguish away from his attention, and he said to the Irsk in front of him, "May I speak?"

The dyl gazed at him, unsmiling and unfriendly by the standards that Bray knew. Then he looked past the prisoner. He called, "Marriott, is this one Colonel Charles Morton?"

Morton, who had been watching the travail of the new arrivals through the eyes of Marriott, said into that individual's mind, "Now don't you betray him. I'm sure the Mahala System is actually out to destroy the true Colonel Charles Morton; so the best defense is simply to keep a confusion going."

Having spoken, he waited anxiously.

Marriott walked forward and stood in front of Bray. There was a grim smile on his face, and unquestionably he recognized the young lieutenant who had come to the Capodochino Corapo post a few nights earlier.

But he turned presently to the Irsk leader and said, "As you know, I'm a scientist; so I can't give you a positive answer. In Colonel Charles Morton, we are dealing with the chief of Intelligence of the Negotiating Committee. So here's what I know."

He thereupon described accurately his meetings with Morton and Bray, concluding, "I have only their statements as to who they are. If this man says he is Colonel Charles Morton, I have no proof one way or the other to determine if it is or is not so."

Whereupon he walked back to the stretcher containing Isolina. As he did so, the real Morton said into Marriott's brain, "Thank you. I couldn't have done it better myself."

"I have a simple principle," Marriott whispered back. "When dealing with Irsk or Diamondians the truth is always the best confuser."

There was an overlong silence. The Irsk leader seemed to be blank. Abruptly, he came to and made a gesture. A tentacle shoved Bray roughly. As earlier, he fell and was caught and lifted into his stretcher again.

The dyl made a second motion. Bray was carried across the room and dumped beside the woman with a violence that jarred his whole body. "Take a look at him, Miss Ferraris. Is this the man whom you knew as Colonel Charles Morton?"

The woman turned her head—and it was she all right: Isolina. She surveyed him in a deliberate fashion. Then she shook her head. "I first knew this man as Lieutenant Lester Bray."

Bray lay where he had been thrown because, physically, there was nothing else for him to do. But he was suddenly intensely excited. These people were saying their truth; yet it did not affect the situation he sensed. Remembering what Morton had said about the entire Diamondian dilemma having the appearance of a puzzle, he *had* to test if that were true.

He glanced over at Kirk and called out, "Kirk, tell them who I am."

The Irsk leader followed his gaze. But it was evident he could not decide for whom the words were meant. For he said, "Whom are you addressing?"

"The young man on the floor in the stretcher."

The leader spoke to Kirk. "What is your name?" he asked.

"I am Colonel Charles Morton," was the steady-voiced reply. As Kirk spoke, he looked at Bray without blinking.

Silently the Irsk leader glided over to Kirk's stretcher. The dyl bent down. "And who is that?" he asked. With one tentacle he pointed at Bray.

Such a question seemed no problem to David Kirk. He answered at once in a clear voice, "That is David Kirk, a special aide of the Intelligence department."

A pause, a sort of silence . . . that ended—

Suddenly, several Irsk shouted something at their leader. He shouted back.

At the big table, the Diamondians became excited. There was a sound of gabbling, and the sight of gesturing.

Words came through from both groups. Something about: "But this is an impossible situation. All these people claiming to be somebody else."

The Irsk leader was the first to recover. He straightened suddenly and seemed to be listening. Then: "Two ambulance attendants," he said, "are bringing the unconscious body of a third Colonel Charles Morton. I have told them to enter."

At least a minute went by. There was some foot shuffling, a few Diamondian whispers, the vague hum of distant machinery. And then—

The door through which Bray and his companions had been brought a short time before opened. The two Irsk ambulance attendants entered, carrying a stretcher on which lay the body of a man in uniform. Morton, watching in puzzlement through the eyes of Marriott, found himself studying a familiar form. What slowed his reaction was the absolute uniqueness of his viewpoint . . . Not a film view nor a mirror reflection, but his *self* looking at—

Mental blankness!

Somebody called an ambulance, was his first thought, finally. And of course that kind of work was still done exclusively by Irsk. The two ambulance attendants, who continued to transport his body across the large room, wore the green-striped coats which signified that they were Friends of the Diamondian People. Morton considered that gloomily; all those millions of green-striped Irsk out there permeating every walk of Diamondian existence.

. . . And they were accepted because they worked. It was better, from the Diamondian point of view, to have somebody who was willing to do that and hope it was all right, than for a Diamondian to condescend to do the work himself.

149

Would all these Irsk in the green-striped friendship shirts and coats suddenly turn on those who trusted them?

He asked Marriott.

The physicist whispered. "No Irsk is completely outside the Irsk community. They all use many of the services. So, I imagine, when you were accidentally handed over to them, they put through a routine check, asking what about Colonel Charles Morton. And of course there was a lot about him—"

Morton said, "The logic of this situation, as I see it, requires that I get back into my own body. Otherwise, they'll guess that it's the real Morton, because obviously the duplicate is off somewhere. Before I go, there's one thing more I should tell you—"

He described what he knew about the Lositeen Weapon taking over the control center of the darkness, finished, "Whatever you have in mind as between you and me will have to take that into account."

To his complete amazement, Marriott was relieved. "Thank God," the man whispered. "That explains the limited things that are being done against this planet. I've been expecting the Mahala to blast the whole place, but the Lositeen Weapon was designed as a second control. It's not on Man's side or on Irsk's side, but it is programmed."

"Then it's no problem?"

"I'll handle it," said Marriott, "With one hand tied behind my back."

No question, thought Morton, here is the man who should be commander in the crisis. Once more he felt impressed. And once more, uneasy. *Damn it, I wish I could trust this genius.* Unquestionably, that was what Marriott seemed to be.

He spoke again, "It's all right if I leave?"

"I," whispered Marriott, "was trying to figure out where to put you while I did something I don't want you to know about. Your own body is definitely the best place. Under the circumstances, you don't need to come back."

Perfect. Black and white. Puzzle level certainties. However, on his way back to his body Morton made an intermediate stop.

Thirty-Five

THIS, HE THOUGHT, is probably my final opportunity to save Isolina.

So he mind-brothered with her . . . and said, "This is Colonel Charles Morton. Don't act surprised. If you wish to speak to me, whisper."

Under him, around him, through him the woman's body stiffened. But mercifully, she had her usual quick wits. She simply waited.

"Isolina," Morton continued, "things are moving fast. So I have to come straight to the point. Will you marry me? Right now? In your heart from this moment forth consider yourself Mrs. Colonel Charles Morton? Whisper your reply."

"For the sake of God," Isolina Ferraris said in a shaking sotto voice, "what kind of a joke is that under these conditions?"

"There's something about your intelligence that attracts me very much," said Morton. "So I ask myself, why should I marry a dull woman? Why not a bright one?"

"But at least four hundred men have had me," she faltered.

"I figured it closer to eight hundred," said Morton lightly. He added, "Would you be faithful to me if we got married?"

"Totally"—her whisper included heavy breathing—"with all my heart, from this moment I am yours alone. No other man than you shall ever possess me again."

"That's good enough for me," said Morton. "So let's consider it settled. But now, one more thing . . . and don't miss a word of this. There's a little restaurant a block inland from the ocean, south of the palace where the Negotiating Committee has its offices. The restaurant is called the Turin. If anything ever happens whereby you and I lose touch with each other, wait for me there any morning at ten o'clock."

Once more the woman lay very still. "That," she whispered, "is the most fantastic piece of information I have ever been given. It seems to be utterly a non sequitur."

"It will be important," said Morton, "only if I have succeeded in getting you confused in somebody's mind with me. Remember the name: the Turin."

Morton decided not to be ashamed of himself. It could be,

he told himself, that I might feel all those things for her—but for the moment the fact was that Mrs. Colonel Charles Morton might conceivably fit into the Morton "set."

If she didn't, or if for some reason she couldn't in her mind accept the new identity, then it was very likely that she was doomed.

Having spoken his final words to her, Morton wasted no time. He did the illusion thing as between the duplicate and his own body.

He left behind him a woman in a totally Diamondian condition of female turmoil.

Naturally, she dismissed the reality of a marriage made purely in a man's mind.

Usually so alert and intent on immediate business, during the entire development—which now occurred elsewhere in the great room—her mind was busy with marital planning. Undoubtedly some of the words spoken by both Irsk and the human beings registered in her sharp brain. But the proposal had figuratively struck her a mortal blow.

Out went her patriotism. Down into nothingness her role as a behind-the-scene leader. Off into vagueness her loyalty to her associates. Forgotten the probable fate of Diamondian people. Reigning supreme, the possibility of marriage in spite of all that she had done.

. . . It was the fateful Diamondian woman syndrome; and she had been sucked into it while her intelligence was looking elsewhere.

By the time it looked back, it had nothing else to do but participate in one mad scheme after another.

Thirty-Six

In New Naples, it was nearly eight o'clock.

Sergeant Struthers sat disconsolately in his office. He had remained on duty because he was a badly worried man. He told himself: Surely the phone will ring any minute, and it will be Lieutenant Bray or Colonel Morton.

As he had that thought for the dozenth time in a half-dozen minutes, the building underneath him moved.

Struthers was an experienced man; and he thought it was an earthquake. He dove under his steel desk—

152

Special instruments in the nearby university later reported that a magnetic field formed around one rear portion of the palace. The field was so intense that the massive steel beams holding up the underlying structure of concrete, wood, and stone were wrenched upward a full ten feet.

As suddenly as the field had formed, it ceased. At once four stories of building crashed ten feet.

In that fall most of the steel beams merely bent. Here and there, entire segments of the building fell down into place relatively intact. But only here and there. All the rest of the rear of the building crashed, crumbled, shattered.

One of the nine men who was later found alive was Struthers. . . .

Eight o'clock. . . . The former Dr. Fondier's clinic (in which he planned to practice under the name, Dr. Colonel Charles Morton) was a thin, one-story building with a narrow front and long rear. He had owned the place for years. It was a haven where he could go in those numerous moments of stress to which Diamondian males are subject. And of course it was fitted out like a doctor's office.

In the rear there was a room fixed up somewhat luxuriously for the convenience of potential private patients who needed to lie down. Being secretly a kindly person, the apoplectic head of the Hospital for the Incuribili had long formed the habit of inviting certain poor girls of the street to use the bed of this rear room for daytime sleeping. And if by chance the weary prostitute found the good-hearted doctor in the bed without any clothes on, well, after all, a Diamondian physician had to go somewhere when he was not in his office at the hospital, which was a lot of the time.

On this first evening of the clinic's operation under its new directive, several patients were attracted by a sign on the door, which read: FREE TREATMENT. At eight o'clock they had already been waiting for nearly an hour in the anteroom.

As a result, they were to a degree witnesses when the entire block of old buildings across the street from the clinic suddenly shuddered, lifted (foundations and all) and took off into the sky.

Literally. Up into the air leaped three-story, four story and two-story structures. Being rickety with age, the basic metal almost at once began to shed floors, ceilings, walls, furniture and people in a roaring combination of screeching wood, thudding everything and screaming men and women.

A thick cloud of plaster and other dust drifted into or descended on the Dr. Fondier-Colonel Charles Morton clinic. The patients there abruptly forgot their aches and departed. As for the doctor himself, naturally—after putting up the sign—he had, like any Diamondian male, promptly found that he had business elsewhere. So he was not even in the place at the time of the disaster.

Fondier's clinic was the second closest strike that the darkness managed against *any* Colonel Charles Morton. The others consisted of a series of attacks aimed at some three hundred other Colonel Mortons during a time period of about twenty-five minutes. In every instance, the wreckage was fearful. On each hit the number of people killed was . . . hundreds. But, in fact, they all missed their targets by ten blocks or more. And so, most of the false Mortons didn't know of the catastrophes until later. And none even suspected that they had been the intended victims of an attacker who normally couldn't hit anything smaller than a mountain.

At 8:22 p.m. New Naples time the massive destruction ceased as suddenly as it had begun.

. . . A few minutes before eight o'clock, Morton opened his eyes in his own body. He was lying on his back and directly above him was a brilliant chandelier, which moved even as he looked at it. At least it seemed to move. The reason, it turned out, what that he was still on a stretcher and still being transported.

He had a thought, then, about faraway Earth, and of his mother and sister in the family home. Undoubtedly they would be alarmed if they could see their Charles now. He felt alarmed, also. Yet even in the most severe crisis of his life, he had never really given time to regrets. During the several dozen seconds that now elapsed as he was carried across the huge main room of the spaceship, he recovered what he had often called his "military" courage. Which was an inward stiffening substance of a different order than the biological stuff of a civilian.

But it was also true that he was able to brace himself because he believed something that none of these others did . . . modern logic, he thought, for this night alone—or maybe for at least five days—you shall exist just as if mathematical sets are real and people are interchangeable.

As he completed that silent reaffirmation, his stretcher was lowered to the floor in front of the dyl who acted as if he were the leader of the merciless killers. Morton had the feeling that unnecessary delays were about to take place. His truth was that Marriott and he ought to be doing something and doing it quickly.

Highly disturbed by that awareness, he nevertheless contained himself, and addressed the Irsk "king." "Mgdabltt," he said, "very important things are happening. We need a very urgent discussion."

The Irsk stared at him with frozen blue gaze. "When did you come to? You were unconscious until a few moments ago." He stopped, stiffened, said grimly, "I will thank you not use the shorted Diamondian version of my name."

"I beg your pardon," said Morton. But he groaned inwardly. He respected these long, original Irsk names. He believed that they had sharpened what was left of Irsk individuality. But this was not the moment.

"Mugadaaabeebeelatata," he said hesitantly, "I consider it extremely advisable that I turn back control of the darkness to Marriott immediately. He has a method where by this can be done, and I should like you to facilitate his take-over. Will you do so? Afterward, we can have a discussion."

A piercing Irsk voice from the rear of the group of Irsk interrupted at that exact moment. The voice said, "I don't think there is any longer any doubt. He is the real Colonel Charles Morton."

Morton blinked. It was a matter at issue that he had almost forgotten. He had to go back in his mind and think and then realize that Irsk were kind of dumb and were slow at understanding these things. And here was that problem again.

Before he could say anything, the leader whirled on the interrupter. "Water in your mouth," he yelled.

"That's easy to say," the answer came back, "but you didn't discover Diamondia either."

The leader screamed something back at the critic and was screamed at in turn.

Morton stared anxiously at the two insane creatures as they shouted at each other. The argument was about him; and *that* he had to take account of.

Hastily, he cast about for a way to divert the excitement that was now beginning to show in every part of the room. The Irsk were waving their tentacles. And all the Diamondians were on their feet now.

Seeing them, he thought: Of course, it's what we're here fore. . . . The best diversion of all was truth.

Urgently, then, he waited. Uneasily, he watched. And then—called out, "We're all drowning in a glass of water. So it's time to have that peace meeting."

155

The Irsk leader did not even seem to notice that it was a different person. He whirled; and his passion now poured down upon Morton. "We Irsk," he shouted, "have been to Canossa for over three hundred years eating Diamondian garbage."

"That will never be true again," said Morton, "but all Irsk are quicksilver now, just like the worst Diamondians."

"You're washing the donkey's head," was the bitter reply, "and you weren't asked. We don't need your help."

"I'm in the dance whether I like it or not. I'm a member of the Negotiating Committee."

"We're feeding you beard and hair. Why don't you people go back where you came from?"

"I cannot unload the barrel that easy. My job is to finish making the goose's beak."

"You've shown no bump for solving problems. The whole Negotiating Committee is at half mouth all the time."

"Our job is to give one blow to the hoop and one to the cask and no one wants to talk to us on these terms."

"You act like you're in an iron cask; as if equality is a fair solution."

"The cask gives the wine it has."

The opportunity that occurred after Morton spoke these words was a logical consequence. Everything he had said, though shouted, was without inner passion. Whereas Mgdabltt visibly was in a state. Abruptly, he literally choked with that emotion. And there was between them a measurable silence.

Into that stillness Morton projected loud and clear his own entire peace thought for Diamondia.

"All right," he yelled, "let's look truth in the eye. Irsk get total control of all those portions of Diamondia known as the hotlands. Diamondians get the mountains and the adjoining seashores. The green-striped Irsk get to stay where they are, or they can move if they wish."

As those words completed, there was the sound of a collective screech.

A pale Morton presently realized that the sound had shrilled simultaneously from every Irsk and from every Diamondian throat.

Total objection. Outrage. Stupid. Who did he think they were?—children!

Morton didn't take time to find out what kind of an S.O.B. they considered him.

He had achieved his diversion.

Even more important, for possibly the first time in Irsk-Diamondian history, somebody had managed to finish stating a set of peace terms. Incredibly, in this entire murderous decade, so violent was everybody's anger, no one had ever been able to suggest publicly that the territorial lines between the two contending parties be drawn on the basis of the status quo.

That he had now done and simultaneously he had gained the opportunity that he needed. On two sides of him were screaming voices, busy with each other and themselves. Morton chose it as a moment to mind-brother with Marriott. "Can we begin?" he said. "I have a feeling that thing up there is doing its damnedest to locate and kill me, and that it won't stop until it succeeds or we get it under control. For the sake of God, act."

Whereupon he returned to his own body.

Lying there, he was greatly relieved to see that Marriott was walking over to Mgdabltt. It took a while even for him to gain the attention of the Irsk leader. Yet, finally, they held a low-voiced conversation. As this progressed, the Irsk delegation began to calm down and was soon silent. It took longer with the Diamondians. But when Marriott presently came to where Morton lay helpless, he seemed to have his audience in hand.

He raised an arm and beckoned Dr. Gerhardt and Lositeen. The psychiatrist walked over in his neutral way. Lositeen came quietly. His eyes stared through Morton when he glanced down and not really at him. Marriott untied Gerhardt. And then the thin-faced, dark-haired man produced the hypnotic gun from his inside breast pocket and handed it to Gerhardt. "I got this from Zoolanyt. I want you to hypnotize these two people—first Lositeen."

The bespectacled man said that Lositeen was already under. "What do you want?" he asked evenly.

"Put him in my control," said a grimly smiling Marriott, "and I'll whisper the instructions."

He glanced triumphantly at Morton. "It's got to be this way," he said. "I can't let you find out the method."

It was not a problem. As Marriott turned away, Morton closed his eyes, mind-brothered with Lositeen, listened as Marriott whispered, "When I clap my hands, you will come out of your hypnosis and take back control of the Lositeen Weapon. Do you understand?"

"I understand," whispered Lositeen.

"You understand," urged Marriott, "that it's programmed to be under your control?"

157

"I understand that," Lositeen emotionlessly.

Morton hastily detached himself and was in his own body as Marriott turned again to Gerhardt. "Now," the physicist commanded, "use that hypnotizing gun on Colonel Morton."

The words startled Morton. He parted his lips to explain that hypnotizing drugs did not work on him for more than a few seconds. What stopped him for a fateful but small period of time was that, as he raised himself to protest, he caught a glimpse of the Diamondians and the Irsk. He had an intense momentary awareness of gray and blue eyes, abnormally bright, staring at this scene; and he had an anxious awareness: They don't understand what's going on.

Before he could think further, several things happened almost simultaneously.

Gerhardt, in his cold fashion, raised the gun, aimed it at Morton—and pulled only one of the two triggers.

Morton, who had braced himself for a few seconds of chemical shock, felt no reaction at all. It was a startling turn of events; and as Marriott bent down beside him, evidently intending to whisper his hypnotic instructions here also, it was Morton who whispered first: "Marriott—listen! Hypnotism doesn't work on me. How else can this be done? I'm willing."

The shock must have been fantastic.

Obvious from the look that came into the physicist's face that he knew of no other solution.

The color drained from his thin face. As he straightened, he staggered. And he was clearly in an automatic condition, for he clapped his hands in a mechanical fashion near Lositeen's head.

Morton was appalled. *But that releases the darkness from whatever control the Lositeen Weapon is exerting over it.*

Abruptly, *he* had no alternative. He put through his mind the eleven code thoughts that would activate the D.A.R. building in Capodochino Corapo.

Before he could turn the control of the building over to Marriott, the only person who was qualified to guide the building equipment properly, a man in the Diamondian delegation produced a gun and fired it. The bullet knocked the hypnotic syringe instrument out of Gerhardt's fingers. It skittered across to a wall and came to rest beside an open grillwork. A steady, shiny, silvery mist rose up from it and was suctioned into the ventilator behind the grill.

Gerhardt smiled his cold smile.. "I was trying to figure out

158

how to do that, myself," he said aloud to no one in particular.

He had no impulse at all to shake the stinging pain out of his hand. Simply, he stood there. Icily, he waited.

In the village of Capodochino Corapo more than 800 miles away, the D.A.R., the "little" military post that had for all these years been commanded by Captain James Marriott, began to fight.

It was set to battle on Marriott's behalf; and that was the way Luftelet allowed it to operate. His reasoning was that the physicist understood the construction and, in leaving it set in his own favor, had clearly believed that it should be in the control of an expert.

Major Luftelet could only concur with that judgement with every beat of his authoritarian heart.

. . . Marriott's first awareness: he sensed Alpha and Beta wave feedback responses in his own brain. At the first sensation in his brain he raised his head, and a vague, hopeful feeling came.

Recognition was sudden.

The shock of excitement brought an instant, huge, wonderful conviction that he might still be able to snatch victory from defeat. . . . *This will hold off the darkness during the time I need.*

Even as he had that thought, he was heading, running, for the door that would take him out of the ship to ground level. Since he was everybody's friend, no one tried to stop him.

But his departure caused consternation and confusion.

Everybody froze. In a space of time no longer than a few seconds, the tableau held. During that time, Morton recovered. And saw that the man with the gun was standing near the center of the table and behind it, of course. Who was he? What was his rank in the delegation. What did he look like?

He looked like a Diamondian. No other identification needed, and no time to make any other.

The Irsk delegation chose that moment to retreat several steps. What the movement of so many individuals meant was naturally not visible to the Diamondians.

In the human delegation, each man, including the leaders, dove for some portion of his baggage or reached into some part of his clothing. Almost as one, each man produced *his* concealed weapon. All thirty odd of them seemed suddenly oblivious of their purpose in being in the ship.

With a crash the table was tipped over. Into its shelter they dove or ducked or crouched or knelt.

After a very few seconds, nothing was moving. All the Irsk had got the hell out of there. They literally dissoved in their gliding fashion through the open doors behind them. . . . Morton caught a glimpse of Lositeen heading for a distant outer door. Of Marriott there was no sign.

During the confusion a number of guns went off—impossible to detect whose. But there was the sinister sound of several other bullets ricocheting in an unfortunate, tuneful fashion from metal walls and unbreakable plastic.

As Morton watched helpless, people did intensely people things. He lay there as vulnerable to stray shots as anyone and noticed that a Diamondian colonel was crawling out from behind the table. The man went over to David Kirk. He produced a knife, turned Kirk over on his face, and cut his bonds. The young man sat up, rubbed his wrists and then asked for the knife. The Diamondian officer unhesitatingly surrendered it.

Kirk hurried over to Bray and cut him loose. Instants later the two men came running toward Morton, who shook his head. "I'm handcuffed," he said regretfully, and added quickly, "Free Miss Ferraris."

They were unbelieving. They turned him over and looked; and there was no question. A knife could not free him from the metal that bound his wrists.

At Bray's gesture, Kirk went off with the knife to Isolina. Hastily the young lieutenant whispered in the ear of his boss what had happened out there in the ravine—his meeting with the Mahala duplicate. He described what it had said.

By the time that was done, Kirk was back. There was a disturbed expression on his face. "She's been hit," he said. "Blood is seeping through in the stomach area."

Even as he spoke, a moaning cry came from the woman. She spoke in a strained voice, "Help me, somebody."

It was Bray who went over this time. He knelt beside her. Then he stood up and came back, pale. "Dr. Gerhardt," he said, "is there anything you can do?"

The psychiatrist went over. Without getting up, Gerhardt turned and called out, "Where are those ambulance attendants?"

Lieutenant Lester Bray said, "I'll get them.."

He was already running for the doors when Morton realized his intent. "Bray," he yelled, "come back here. You'll be killed."

Without a backward glance, as if he had not heard, the

young officer continued on through one of the open doors beyond which the main body of Irsk had retreated.

A minute went by. Two. Three.

The woman ceased her sobbing. She said, "Crying does no good, and pain can be endured silently."

She turned her head. Her eyes, almost as large and moist as an Irsk's, and as mistily blue, gazed at Morton. "Charles," she said, "what's going to happen to the Diamondian people?"

Morton couldn't answer. The disaster had struck so suddenly that he was still in his own state of shock. He asked, "Where are you hit?"

Her impression: the bullet had pierced the lower abdomen and shattered a bone.

Death! He sensed it.

It was a special darkness in him because it had been so unnecessary. He could feel the modern logic rage swelling up inside him. . . . But he noticed it, and it went away.

What bothered him was that there was something he should be doing as a consequence of what Bray had told him. Instead he said to Kirk, "Carry me over to her."

Kirk and one of the Diamondians picked up his stretcher and deposited it a few moments later about two feet from where the woman lay.

During that brief interval she had had her sudden Diamondian woman's thought: "While I am hurt like this, it will be a pushover for me to get him to marry me. . . ."

Yes, she had thought. She believed she was dying, but that deep need took over and made either an idiot or a genius out of her. She felt no shame, no consciousness of what an out of proportion impulse it was to have such a purpose in such a condition.

With the sudden, shocking impact and the feeling of her body defiled by a deadly intruder, what remained of her good sense drained out of her with her dripping blood. She made the request of Morton with a total simplicity, "Charles, I should like to die Mrs. Charles Morton."

"Mrs. *Colonel* Charles Morton," corrected Morton.

The priest, who had accompanied the Diamondian peace mission, performed the marriage in a perfunctory fashion. Morton, who had been present at his mother's second wedding on Earth, recognized the attitude. A Catholic priest marrying a Catholic to a non-Catholic, simply did his minimum task. It was not a marriage of heaven, was his visible posture.

161

The marriage ceremony completed.

About thirty more seconds went by.

Bray came in by the same door as he had gone. With him was one of the ambulance attendants.

Afterward, Morton remembered the attendant kneeling beside Isolina; and he recalled saying to Bray. "I'm going to try to mind-brother with that Mahala duplicate. Wish me luck!"

And he recalled noticing that there was a sparkling mist in the air around him. Abruptly he was motivated to make the effort to save one more person. He yelled at Gerhardt. "From this moment on, you are Colonel Charles Morton—"

Thirty-Seven

A PARTIAL EXODUS of wild life from the Gyuma Ravine had begun shortly after the first hostilities between Diamondian and Irsk main forces. That first evening, the firing of guns had merely tautened nerves and stiffened muscles. A few pigeons, having had the experience of being fired upon while migrating earlier in the season, had flown off toward the setting sun just before nightfall. And two comb-ducks had deserted their tree roosts and headed north.

That was the extent of the first day's migration.

Oddly, the unnerving shot for most of the birds was the one fired at night by Joaquin at the crocodile. It made them tense and uneasy. Some night-flying snipe departed immediately, but the next group of pigeons did not leave until the burst of rifle fire that broke the silence shortly after sunup.

The Silver and Kalij pheasants, strong runners, did not trouble to fly. They headed stealthily through the jungle toward the grassy plain at the south of the ravine.

A female pheasant came unexpectedly upon a Diamondian paratrooper crouching beside a stone. It had its neck wrung before it could even start to utter its *how-owoo* cry.

That was the only casualty then.

As the first shots echoed on the morning air, the two leapards stirred restlessly on their grassy couches. Then, of one accord, they rose and slunk off to the south. Both were furious.

None of the smaller jungle cats, and not a single squirrel,

badger or otter did more than leave the immediate vicinity of the loud, sharp sounds. A cat-bear that had climbed down into the ravine during the night, climbed out again and lumbered off eastward.

Throughout the day, as the intermittent firing continued, most of the animals, merely moved from where the sharp cracking sounds of Diamondian rifle fire was loudest. The ravine was their home, and they really had nowhere else to go. And so, like the peasants of other days and other planets, they crouched in their little homes—under a log, inside a natural cave, or in a burrow—while the armies surged back and forth over them.

The Diamondian paratroopers took the trouble to shoot at every animal or bird they saw. And so as the hours ground on, a certain number of animals were killed, or, worse, wounded.

By the second night the wildlife was in a bad state of unsettlement. Every creature was unhappy. Many were grief stricken, and some, like the leopards, were continuously angry. The big animals lay with lashing tails, ready to attack, but not knowing where or at what the charge should be made, the claws should slash and the teeth should tear.

On this third night the man who ran down the trail was blind to the jungle and its creatures. So long accustomed to civilization, the reality of the animal life was as remote for his scheming brain as it would normally be to a lifetime urban dweller.

His fear was that those he had left behind him in the ship would pursue him and would catch him before he got to the little, buried blockhouse that he had built there shortly after he schemed his great scheme of taking over the giant power in the sky for himself . . .

Why should men die for causes? . . . It was a question Marriott had asked himself often. And answered that there was no reason.

Ten hours before, seeing the gentle Irsk turn into assassins hurt him. Yet he could not bring himself to let go of the power that was causing the disturbance in the Mahala System.

So then he knew why.

The drive toward absolute ascendancy . . . I will not give it up.

He had accordingly long ago made his peace with his own madness, as other tyrants had done before him. So he knew what he must do.

In the blockhouse, he would climb aboard an aircraft. As he took off in it, his departure would trigger a nuclear bomb.

How much of the immediate vicinity and how many people and animals would it blow up? He didn't care. Only *his* skin mattered. Nobody else's. Only he was real to himself. Other people were shadows, who would disappear sooner or later. So why not now?

The two leopards made no sound as they darted down. The man had one terrified half glimpse of a large cat face, with its glinting yellow eyes, and a dim awareness of oversize teeth bared.

Death is not really painful when it is delivered by razor claws and teeth that can crunch a neck or a shoulder in a single slash. The male attacked first, but the female was so close behind that the two leopards literally tore the body apart in forty-five seconds.

They ceased their ripping and biting, when they suddenly saw the luminous figure coming along the pathway. Snarl, rage, animal madness—they turned, and after the so many and the so swift noises of the massacre, they were gone into the darkness.

The being, who did not resemble either an Irsk or a human, was taller than both by at least a foot. His head, though not manlike at all, was egg shaped. The transparency of him had a silvery sheen to it.

In those first moments the impression of a leonine head was very strong. His eyes were wide apart, round and golden in color. If he had ears, they were not located at the sides of that noble head. He looked supremely intelligent, sensitive, perceptive and aware—but different.

He walked out of the nothingness onto the trail where the dead body lay. Already a jackal had come up. It now sat and stared up at the intruder with eyes that were as yellow in their own primitive fashion as the luminous being's were civilized gold—

Morton, mind-brothered with that luminous being, said, "How can we establish a relationship whereby the human race, the Irsk and the Mahala System can live peacefully together?"

The alien replied, "I have no authority to make such an agreement.

"My original Self," said the being, "will return here in about two thousand more years. You can discuss it then."

"If that's your final answer," said Morton, "then I shall have to hold over control of you with Marriott's method."

164

"I need your permission to consult the nearest local area. It will take a while."

"Then take that while," said Morton, "take my permission and talk to me later."

He withdrew.

Thirty-Eight

IT WAS NIGHT.

Lieutenant Lester Bray walked into the front entrance of the Committee palace without noticing that the rear section of the building was almost totally demolished. Exactly how he had got to New Naples was not clear to him. His overall confusion included thoughts unrelated to anything he had ever considered before. And he was dimly aware that somewhere he had lost his uniform and was now dressed in some kind of pants and shirt.

Some of his wits remained. Being Bray, he nodded casually at the guard, said, "Hello, Pete!" and started to walk on as if he were one of the civilian employees.

"Wait a minute, you," said the large man at the desk, and he said it in a voice that began on a note of surprise and ended in a yell.

Bray stopped, shrugging.

"Who are you?" the guard bellowed.

Really, thought Bray, does he have to be that loud about it? He turned in a pained fashion, but he supposed that, in truth, he had never been known to any of these men and had merely got by in the past because he wore the magic uniform. Quietly, he gave his name, finished, "It just happens that I am wearing civvies tonight, so if you'll excuse me—" Once more he turned to go.

As he did so, two soldiers came charging out of a door a few feet down the hall, a door which had a light above it, and a sign which read: "Officer of the Guard." The two men grabbed Bray and brought him back to the desk.

Moments later an Earth federation lieutenant emerged from the guardroom. "What's the problem?" he asked. "You buzzed."

The big man pointed at Bray. "This Diamondian says he's Lieutenant Lester Bray."

Involuntarily, Bray glanced around for whoever was being referred to. Saw no one. For once he was not quick enough. "What Diamondian?" he asked.

"*You!*"

. . . At six a.m., he was interviewed by the ambassador extraordinary, who said, "By this time you probably realize that you are a Diamondian male, not in uniform, about thirty-two years of age; and that according to the identification in your billfold your name is Pierre Magnan.

"Now, here," Laurent picked up some papers, "I have a printout of the movements of Lieutenant Lester Bray, and they are pretty fantastic. But the final record on him shows that he was on a plane that landed on the edge of Gyuma Ravine two nights ago. Apparently he was at that time a prisoner and in a state of chemically induced hypnosis."

"That is correct, sir. I was there with Dr. Gerhardt, a green-striped Irsk named Lositeen and a rebel Irsk named Zoolanyt—whom I didn't see again after we got to our destination. We were taken into a ship, and just about the last thing I remember is Colonel Morton being brought in on a stretcher. He was tied hand and foot." He broke off, "As for the hypnosis, naturally, with my Intelligence training, I deconditioned myself on that, and it was never a factor."

Laurent picked up another paper, glanced at it, and then looked up and said, "An Earth federation officer with the rank of major last night entered the hospital where Dr. Gerhardt works and went straight to Gerhardt's office. He was arrested, but he kept insisting that he *was* Dr. Gerhardt. . . . And then, here," the slender fingers touched another paper, "a Diamondian prostitute came in last night shortly after you arrived and said that she was David Kirk. At first the guard thought she wanted to visit Kirk, which," a wan smile, "would have been more reasonable. But she insisted. And so she is also being held, pending further investigation."

Laurent spread his beautiful hands, helplessly. "What do you make of all this, uh, lieutenant?"

During those minutes the Bray spirit had surfaced. "I think, sir, we'd better get Kirk, Gerhardt and myself together and see what we can reason out," said Bray.

Laurent thought that was an excellent idea. He hesitated; then: "I have a report here from Major Luftelet. He says that beginning at 8:22 last night the building over there fought a battle with the magnetic field which surrounds Diamondia. How does that timing fit in?"

The two men stared at each other. Bray gulped finally, "That would be about right, sir. . . . What happened?"

"Well, if I understand Luftelet correctly, which," Laurent added, "is not always easy to do, the battle lasted a fraction under eight and three quarter minutes, which, according to Luftelet, is within one il of the building's finite logic number."

"Then the building won?"

"Luftelet," said Laurent, "is preparing a report—but I have to say this, lieutenant, when I look at what happened to you, I can't quite accept that the building's victory was—total. In fact, following tracer lines on Colonel Morton and Lieutenant Bray, I have dispatched one of our special units to the Gyuma Ravine. They reported in a few minutes ago and said they have detected a large object underground beside a cliff. We may deduce that this is the spaceship to which you referred. Attempts to communicate with those aboard have not been successful. The expedition is proceeding cautiously."

A brief silence on Bray's part. Then he said in a low voice, "No word in all this from or about Colonel Morton?"

"None."

Thirty-Nine

MORTON WATCHED the strange girl as she came uncertainly into the restaurant. Abruptly satisfied, he walked over to her. "Isolina?" he said.

She was a slim, young creature with jet black hair, and a face that was normally quite bold. Not now. Now the eyes stared at him, startled. "Yes," she breathed, "but who are you?"

He smiled a thick, greasy smile "Right now," he said, "according to a mirror that I shudderingly looked into a while back, I'm a thick-lipped, wide-faced, brown-eyed, oily-skinned, chunkily built Diamondian about five feet six inches tall. But I'm a kind of a cheerful guy who owns a small business in the old part of the city and has a wife who is thin and tall and bitter, because I don't always show up at night when she thinks I should. But being a Diamondian male, I shrug off her words. I've got her fairly well tamed, and I'm happy. But," he finished, showing a mouthful of white teeth in an ingratiating smile, "I'm really Colonel Charles Morton."

"Charles," said the girl tensely, "what's happened?"

Morton's heavy, pawlike hand caught her arm, urged her forward into the restaurant. "Let's have breakfast," he said. "I have a billfold with money in it, so we can splurge."

It was a small place with a dozen booths, of which only three were occupied. The two Diamondian types—the small heavy man and the slender girl—settled into one of the unoccupieds. When they were seated, Morton smiled at the young woman across from him and said, "You made out pretty good." He pursed his lips, surveyed her critically. "Hmm, nineteen and a half, very black hair, finely formed face and that's a streamlined body if ever I saw one. You could live with that getup." He finished, "Considering that Diamondian men are among the handsomest anywhere, I didn't do so well."

"Stop this nonsense!" said Isolina. "What is all this?"

"Modern logic."

She stared at him blankly.

Morton said simply, "The concept of interchangeable parts carried over to people."

She continued to gaze at him, clearly not understanding and definitely not happy.

Morton said, "Today, you're—what is your name?" He pointed at her purse. "Have you opened that?"

"Yes. I'm a prostitute with the name of Maria—Maria Castagna."

"Maria?" Morton winced, then shrugged his thick shoulders. "I suppose that could make it even simpler. This planet has Marias by the jillion. Right now about five thousand prostitutes with that or a similar name and an equal number of males—evenly divided between Earth federation officers and Diamondians like me—are interchangeable with you and me."

"How is this . . . modern logic?"

Morton explained patiently that the ten thousand were now all like so many transistor tubes of the same number. "We're all UT-Ols, as an example. *We* can see with our infinite logic awareness that there's a difference, but the darkness has got us all lumped together." Once more, he smiled his bog-toothed smile, shrugged. "Nobody ever said that modern logic didn't work. It's just limited to jamming similar objects in to do each other's work. Seems to be all right, doesn't it?"

"For the sake of God," said Isolina, "how can you take it so lightly?"

"As the old saying goes," said Morton, "I'm living with the world as it sometimes is."

"But where's my real body?" the girl demanded. Her voice was suddenly angry; and the waitress, who had just brought their order, pulled away. Maria-Isolina drew back and sat gazing off into space. When the woman had finally gone, the girl said in a somewhat more tearful voice, "Where is it?"

Morton stared at her grimly. "I was hoping to get a few facts from you," he said. "What's your last memory?"

"The last thing I remember," the girl said, "is Marriott and the Irsk running out of those doors." She stopped, her liquid brown eyes widening. "What could have made them do such a thing?" she asked, astonished.

Morton said, "Now, think hard. Do you remember the marriage ceremony?"

The black-haired girl's face twisted with the effort of trying to recall. Suddenly her eyes widened. "Oh, my God," she said, "You mean that's *real*?"

Morton drew a deep breath of relief. "What you just did there tells me my analysis is correct. You just penetrated a spontaneous amnesia. So that gives me the picture, and we were all very lucky is my guess."

"How do you mean?"

Morton continued, "The bullet that hit the hypnotic syringe knocked it out of Gerhardt's hand over to a ventilator, which sucked in about half a liter of that potent stuff and sent it first to the lower floors, where most of the Irsk went—and I'll bet knocked them out. Coming back, the gas would be held in some tanks, which are not equipped to deal with that kind of pollutant. . . . I know, because Intelligence monitors all such manufacturing and doesn't permit its own techniques to be bypassed. So, presently, the gas circulated back toward us; and even my body, when subjected to a steady dosage, is probably still saturated and therefore not able to throw off the effect automatically. And Lieutenant Bray, also."

"But," she said vaguely, "us . . . here we are."

"We," said Morton, "are a new factor."

She seemed not to hear. "What's going to happen to us?" she said plaintively.

"Whenever you change, meet me here." He nodded his acceptance of the thought. "That should do it," he said. "After all, fifty percent of us are here in New Naples, so the statistics are very favorable."

The liquid brown eyes were staring at him. "What do you mean? What are you talking about?"

"For heaven's sake, Isolina," said Morton, "don't just sit

there like a dumb Diamondian. This is going to go on. There's ten thousand in this circuit. As time goes on we may add to it. Tomorrow you may be in the body of an Earth federation colonel, though so far there's only one of those."

He added apologetically, "I'm sorry I made all the women in the circuit prostitutes, but I couldn't bring myself to include the wonderful, put upon, good Diamondian wives and mothers in the nightmare of the daily or weekly or whatever shift—it'll be fairly rapid. . . . Diamondian men already regard women as interchangeable, so for them it's not—"

He broke off. "Picture us," he urged, "in all this confusion of different bodies, always seeking each other out. Wouldn't you like that?"

Just like that the reality must have finally got to her. Her small, bold face changed. Excitement. She grabbed his wrist. "Oh, my God," she said, "yes, yes." She was suddenly terrified. "We'll have to get a permanent phone number . . . something—"

Morton put his other hand over her hand that clutched him so frantically. "Isolina, calm yourself. We've got one meeting place right here. So we can do all those other things, whatever's necessary, in due course. Are you willing to stay married to me in this situation?"

The girl parted her lips to say yes, and her eyes were suddenly starry—and then, suddenly a shocked expression was on her face. "But tomorrow I'll be a little bitch in New Rome, and you'll be in New Milan or in the front lines with the Earth federation forces—"

"True."

"Surely you put a time limit on all this?"

Morton gazed at her gloomily. "These posthypnotic suggestions don't always work out; so, in order to be absolutely safe, everybody was instructed to contact the S.R.D. after five days, at which time they were to be thoroughly and directly deconditioned."

"What's wrong with that?"

"I was by there early this morning," said Morton. "That whole section of building is destroyed. The computer, being metal, was actually lifted about a hundred feet; and when it fell ten million fuses burned out—"

A strange look came into her face. "Then this could be forever?"

Morton did not reply directly. He held up his hand, shushing her. "Wait!" he breathed, "I've just been tuned in on a fantastic conversation—"

In his brain a lisping voice said, "This is Mahala System A-24-69-73-2 calling Local Prime Universal Area. Reporting an RQD problem. A series of Logic Class happenings have produced a Puzzle Level crisis. And either help or advice is urgently needed."

(Answer: Help is impossible. The A-24 systems are outer rim locations 69 stages beyond direct communication. Proceed, Two!)

The Diamondian Mahala System described events leading up to the Morton confusion, concluded, "What advice do you have?"

(Solution: It was never intended that a control unit should be in a state of identity confusion. Therefore, a 96-T is indicated.)

"Isn't that extreme?"

(Check: first, extermination of species?)

"Failed."

(Check: destruction of control unit original?)

"Defeated by preempting device."

(Solution: 96-T indicated.)

"Very well."

Morton grew dimly aware that the girl was watching him anxiously. "You have a very strange look in your eyes," she said.

"Wait!" admonished Morton. "It's not over."

Forty

A WOMAN'S FAMILIAR VOICE said, "I don't know. I just suddenly felt faint."

Morton turned and walked across a brightly lit kitchen over to a mirror and looked into it. The face that stared back at him (so it couldn't be a mirror) was that of his sister, Barbara. She examined him very closely and then said, "I'm quite pale. No color at all."

And then he got it!

But she's on Earth, he thought. It was a tiny protest that he uttered silently. And it was almost immediately overwhelmed by the fantastic reality. . . . A second enormous thought came: *More than 700 light-years!*

171

Morton thought: This is what Marriott was fighting for: total power, total communication . . . for himself.

During every instant of his conversation with his sister, which he now initiated, his mind was growing, expanding, exploding with the awareness of that meaning.

He said, "Barbara, it's your brother, Charles. I'm speaking to you by a new method, directly into your brain. Sit down somewhere and just talk aloud in your normal voice, and I'll be able to hear."

Even as he uttered those words . . . somewhere . . . he realized that actually for him it was even easier than that. In a way he *was* his sister. As with Lositeen that first time, her thoughts moved through him as if they were his thoughts.

Morton-Barbara ran. It was he running. That's the way it seemed. The two of them (brother-sister) ended up breathless on a cute little breakfast nook bench in the kitchen. Sitting there, Barbara's voice came, "Oh, my God!" she said.

"What's the matter?" said another woman's voice from another room.

Morton said, "Tell her whatever is necessary. I don't know how long this connection will hold."

(It felt fabulously stable.)

The way Barbara handled the interruption: when the middle-aged woman came in, her several inquiries were simply waved into silence.

"Charles, this is incredible!"

It was that all right.

But he had no time for explanations. He said, "It was either call you by Star Transit or this new method." He braced himself and spoke his lie, "It's just a social call, such as I make occasionally—"

Nearly always in the past at some moment of crisis, when he wasn't absolutely sure that things were going to work out, those were his family call times. He said glibly, "All I want to find out is, is everything all right there?—here, that is."

Barbara was recovering. "Where are you calling from?"

"I'm still on Diamondia."

"How's the war going?"

That was easy. "Classified information," he said, and added, "Is mother still with her second husband?"

"Mother," said the sweet, feminine voice, "is the only perfect wife that I've ever met. No thought of suspicion when he stays out all night. Now, me," she said, and her voice was suddenly brittle, "Luke called me yesterday and demanded

172

that I take him back. I told him where he could go." She laughed grimly. "That's *my* marriage."

Morton said. "There are psychiatric suggestions for how a wife should handle the Lukes of this world—"

She interrupted, "I refuse to play games."

"Then," said Morton, "don't even talk to him."

"But I love him." Suddenly tearful.

Morton said hastily, "I've got to break this off, Barbara." He added, wonderingly, "What is there about certain males?"

"I don't know." Bravely, "Goodbye, Charles."

"Goodbye. Say goodbye to mother."

"I will."

The scene there in the kitchen on Earth—so vivid, so totally *real*—vanished.

Nothingness stirred—

And became—

I-you-me-it-everyone . . . became Morton.

Morton was vaguely aware of himself spread across the entire space in and around the sixth planet of the Diamondian sun.

Around him, the world . . . brightened. Points of light; first a few. But increasing. At the beginning they seemed relatively close. They spread farther. Awareness of distance abruptly brought that lightening world into focus; and he saw that he was gazing at the starry universe.

Suddenly, below him, he saw a fantastic sight. A planet that shone up at him with a million lights. . . . But (thought Morton, critically) planets were not like that. They were misty and cloud covered. The atmosphere of an ordinary, inhabited world was like a foggy mist that hid all except the grossest features. Normally, cities at this height were invisible.

But there, all around him, were faintly luminous lines. They reached down to the surface of a large planet below him. The lines were almost invisible. But the overall effect of so *many* was of a solid mass of dim brightness. Morton was trying to think of what the intent was in giving him this colossal view for *so long*—when the entire scene went out of focus. Suddenly he saw double, treble, quadruple.

Instantly his vision centers were strained by the phenomenon. Two planetary surfaces, four, many. The number of light lines also multiplied.

Morton tried to think of the out-of-focus condition as a problem in fusing several visual images. He did eye-squeezing things in the hope of bringing everything back into one piece.

Wouldn't . . . couldn't . . .

I'm being made aware, he thought, that the darkness can see every curving side of the planet at one time and somehow is capable of integrating the whole planet of Diamondia within its perception. Obviously, he couldn't be expected to do that. So what was the problem?

Maybe if he treated each view like an illusion and permitted all the others to go out of focus—

He did it.

Instantly there was a single view of the planet below him. Of the north pole. Deliberately he shifted. This time the scene was of a vast ocean area.

Got it, he thought, triumphant.

As he had that . . . final, as it turned out, visual awareness, Morton began to hear a sound. Voices. Millions of them.

Long ago at college he had tuned into one of those message bundles, which transmitted phone calls over interstellar distances. The principle of using a radio wave as a carrier beam along which the bundles flashed at translight speed had fascinated him, and the method of sending thousands of such calls in one "bundle" was, as his instructor had termed it, "an elegant technique."

Those voices, *then*, with volume low, had made a sound like a vast auditorium filled with people, all talking before the program started.

This was like that, except that here were multi-times more voices.

He thought, awed: Could it be I'm listening in on *all* the conversations going on down there?

The possibilities were too vast for him to confront in one tiny span of time. He wondered if he still had control of his own movements.

In the ambassador's office the ViewComm buzzed. A voice said into the room. "From the search party, sir."

Hastily Laurent picked up the receiver. There was silence as he listened. Finally, with a glance at the Diamondian-Bray, he asked, "And what about the body of Lieutenant Lester Bray? I have someone with me who may be especially interested."

He hung up presently, said with a grave smile, "They only found one person dead: Miss Ferraris."

Laurent broke off. "The rescue crew went in wearing gas masks and found about three score humans and Irsk, all unconscious. The only known person missing was Marriott. It is estimated that half a liter of hypnotizing gas was released,

174

enough to keep everybody out for several days in that confined space."

His white face suddenly had color in it, a cheerful expression. "I'm having them all brought here. I think we should have a peace meeting quickly. And, under the circumstances of all the delegates being under hypnosis, I'm very hopeful. It seems to be the final Absolute of that puzzle aspect you mentioned—"

. . . Morton found himself back in the little restaurant, staring at Maria-Isolina Castagna-Ferraris.

"What happened?" she whispered. "They've come twice with the bill."

Morton said, "Solution 96-T seems to be: the local group is supposed to do as I say—and in about another two thousand years somebody will come by and see if I let happen what they want. I'll have to resign my commission and remain on Diamondia. What do you think? Is it a good idea to let all human beings be interchangeable with Colonel Charles Morton?"

The small, black-haired girl seemed to become progressively more animated as he spoke. Abruptly she jumped to her feet, came around the table and plumped herself onto the lap of the heavyset, swarthy Diamondian.

"It is time," she announced, "that Mr. and Mrs. Colonel Charles Morton went somewhere private and did something affectionate. But," she concluded, "I can tell you one thing."

"What's that?"

"Such a scheme as this Mahala has will never be acceptable to Diamondians."

Having spoken, she kissed him with her dainty mouth squarely on his large, puffy lips.

Epilogue

Earth.

Time: several weeks later.

The assistant editor, after knocking, brought the manuscript into his chief's office and laid it gently down on the great man's desk.

"Got another story from Lieutenant Lester Bray. From Diamondia."

"Hey, that's where that peace treaty has just been signed. Let me see that."

With glistening eyes, he read the opening sentences:

"Gray thoughts under a gray sky. . . . Across the darkening roofs of New Naples, Christomene watched from her window Vesuvius II sputtering and smoking—"

The editor looked up at his junior, his eyes round and happy. "Boy, oh, boy, listen to that local color. We've got to get this into the next issue. We'll scoop the trade with what's practically an eyewitness story from the scene. Right?"

"Right!"